VOL. 2, NO. 1　　　　　　　　　　　　　　　　　　**ISSUE #5**

FEATURES

NEW STORIES

CLASSIC REPRINT

FROM THE CAT'S PERCH

Welcome to the fifth issue of *Black Cat Mystery Magazine*—and the start of a new era here. (Not necessarily *better*, but definitely *new*.) With this issue, I am pleased to welcome Michael Bracken to the staff as our new co-editor, stepping into the very large (but not literally!) shoes of the multi-talented Carla Coupe, who has retired. Her name remains on the masthead this issue, since she helped select the stories.

Where do old editors go? Carla has promised to get back to her writing career (readers of *Black Cat*'s sibling publication, *Sherlock Holmes Mystery Magazine*, will doubtless remember the exceptional stories she published there). We wish her all the best and much continued success. And she better send Michael and lme some of her new tales for *this* magazine!

Michael Bracken is, I trust, already a familiar name to *Black Cat* readers, since his stories have been featured in every issue to date. (His story in this issue continues the trend.) When he first offered to help edit the magazine, my initial reply was an enthusiastic, "Of course! But only if you continue to write for it, too." So rest assured, we won't lost him as an author to gain him as an editor. I will be solely responsible for selecting any fiction he submits, and he will be held to an even higher standard than every other author who submits. Of course, I have faith that he's up to it.

Next issue will be a special Private Eye edition. Meantime, turn the page and enjoy issue 5!

—John Betancourt
Publisher, Wildside Press

Staff

PUBLISHER
John Gregory Betancourt

EDITORS
John Gregory Betancourt and *Michael Bracken* and *Carla Coupe*

WILDSIDE PRESS SUBSCRIPTION SERVICES
Karl Würf

PRODUCTION TEAM
Sam Cooper
Steve Coupe
Shawn Garrett
Yamini Manikoth

THE SHOW MUST GO ON
MICHAEL BRACKEN

The Bearded Lady settled her head upon my pillow and wept. I could neither stroke her hair nor wipe away her tears, so I lay beside her and held her as best I could.

"He did it to me again," she whispered.

There were few secrets among the performers, and we all knew the iron-fisted dwarf who owned Wee Willie's Hall of Human and Animal Oddities, Wondrous World of Prodigies of Physical Phenomena and Living Human Curiosities took advantage of the female members of his traveling show. We all knew and we did nothing.

"He said he would kick me out if I didn't let him," she said. "Where would I go? What would I do?"

Wee Willie had threatened each of us, and we had all asked ourselves the same questions. The Depression had its tentacles wrapped the country, and even the able-bodied clung to whatever work they had. We considered his abuse a small price to pay for three squares a day, though some of us endured much more than others.

During the summer, Wee Willie's show traversed the northern half of the country from Appalachia to the eastern Rockies and then returned through the southern states each winter, offering both a grind show and a ten-in-one, and visiting only rural communities often overlooked by sophisticated traveling shows such as the three-ring circus.

The Hall of Human and Animal Oddities was a grind featuring pickled punks, which were human fetuses preserved in glass jars filled with formaldehyde, each displaying some form of anatomical abnormality. Wee Willie included animal punks in the grind, the most popular being the two-headed hippopotamus, a put-up job cobbled together from a pair of stillborn hippos acquired from a circus traveling a circuit that crossed ours near Lincoln. Though some of the punks were real, or were created from real fetuses and dead animals, an equal number were bouncers—fake pickled punks made from rubber or wax, with weak tea added to the formaldehyde to darken it and obscure their fabricated nature because they could not bear scrutiny.

The Wondrous World of Prodigies of Physical Phenomena and Living Human Curiosities, of which I was a part, offered such prodigies as the Tattooed Woman and the Sword Swallower, and such living human curiosities as the Bearded Lady, the Human Sea Lion, the Two-in-One conjoined Harris twins, and Wee Willie himself, all four-feet-nine-inches of him decked out in top hat and tails and sporting a gold-tipped walking cane he often wielded as a weapon. Should the cane prove insufficient motivation, he also carried a Remington Double Derringer in his waistcoat pocket.

Joyce was gone when I woke the following morning. Though I looked, I couldn't find her anywhere in the backyard where the private trailers for living and storage are hidden from the public behind the main tent. So, I made my way to the cook tent for breakfast. I sat with the Harris twins—fourteen-year-old teenaged girls Wee Willie had purchased for $300 while traveling through Appalachia two years earlier. They were joined at the hip, shared several vital organs, and had recently endured puberty in full view of the other performers.

I drank my breakfast through a straw while they wolfed down bacon and eggs and chattered about a young man they had seen at the previous day's show.

"He winked at me."

"No, he winked at me!"

"No boy would ever wink at you. Your fanny's too big."

"That's only because it's stuck to yours!"

Lettie and Nettie were still giggling when Wee Willie strode into the cook tent. The other performers grew silent, only the sound of their cutlery scraping against their tin plates offering a counter-point to the girls' adolescent peals. He stopped at our table, ogled the twins for a moment as they swallowed their laughter, and then turned to me. "Get ready, Paul. I want you on the bally stand when we open."

Though I knew what Wee Willie had done the previous night, I was no more brave than any of the other performers, unwilling to say or do anything that might draw his ire and send me on the short trip to Tap City. I lowered my gaze to the half-empty glass before me. "Yes, sir."

Wee Willie was not only a performer in the show he owned, he was the showman as well, the talker spinning his patter outside the main tent to convince skeptical rubes to part with hard-earned money. Like Wee Willie, most of the other performers served double-duty. Most helped take down the banner line and pack the tent when we broke down the show, then helped set everything up again at the next stop. Some had other duties. Joyce kept the books and Tina oversaw the Hall of Human and Animal Oddities, ensuring that we always had a sufficient quantity of formaldehyde should we ever encounter something worth adding to the show. Only I did not have secondary responsibilities.

As the Human Sea Lion, born with webbed toes and flipper-like appendages where my arms should have been, I often worked the bally stand while Wee Willie froze the tip. I would slap my flippers together while making a barking noise, balance a beach ball on my nose, and catch in my mouth the pickled herring he tossed in my direction.

After Wee Willie walked away, I slurped down the last of my breakfast, walked to the dressing area behind the main tent to be helped into my costume, and then waited behind the tent flap for Wee Willie to call me to the bally stand. Through the canvas I could hear him building the tip.

"Step right up, ladies and gentlemen, boys and girls! This is the show you've been waiting for all your lives! You've heard about it! You've read about it! You've even dreamed about it! And it's right here, right now! Wee Willie's Hall of Human and Animal Oddities, Wondrous World of Prodigies of Physical Phenomena and Living Human Curiosities!"

I had heard Wee Willie's talk so often I could practically recite it along with him.

"Yes, ladies and gentlemen, boys and girls, I *am* the infamous Wee Willie, small of stature but all man where it counts! I know some of you have already visited the Hall of Human and Animal Oddities, but the sights you beheld there pale in comparison to the sights you'll see inside the tent behind me!"

The talk continued as Wee Willie listed the delights that would be found in the main tent, and before long it was time to freeze the tip.

"And now ladies and gentlemen, boys and girls, I'll give you just a little taste of the Prodigies of Physical Phenomena and Living Human Curiosities to be found inside. Joining us now, a sight so strange as to have never before been seen this far inland, the Human Sea Lion!"

Though I could walk when not costumed, the skin-tight suit I wore covered me from ankle to hip, turning my legs into a single stem, and by balancing myself on my flippers and heaving my legs along, I entered the bally stand, to the delight of the crowd, much as a Sea Lion might have.

Wee Willie pulled a pickled herring from his pocket, tossed it toward me, and I caught it out of the air. He followed that with a beach ball, which I balanced on my nose while I slapped my flippers together, before batting it back to Wee Willie.

Willie tossed another pickled herring and I caught it. As I left the bally, Willie turned the tip.

"Ladies and gentlemen, boys and girls, isn't that just amazing? And that's just one of the many tricks the Human Sea Lion does during his performance inside this tent, one of only ten Prodigies of Physical Phenomena and Living Human Curiosities you will see during the show! Ten performances for the price of one! There are only a few minutes left to purchase your tickets, so get them now! Don't delay! The show's about to start!"

The tent quickly filled and the show began. Joyce had returned in time to be the first performer, and she wore a gown that emphasized her female form. Her act, such as it was, mostly consisted of letting children tug on her beard.

Sally the Sword Swallower, one of Wee Willie's favorites because she had no gag reflex, performed next. Then came the Tattooed Woman and the other performers in turn until I took the stage, balanced the beach ball and a variety of other objects on my nose, and snatched more pickled herring out of the air. I relinquished the audience's attention when Wee Willie began describing an unfamiliar ding, an extra-special added attraction never advertised outside the main tent that could only be viewed by paying an additional fee.

"Ladies, boys, and girls, thank you for joining us today and I hope you can see yourself out, but gentlemen I want to draw your attention to the curtain at the end of the platform, a curtain behind which—" He lowered his voice to a conspiratorial stage whisper, causing the crowd to lean forward to hear. "—behind which is a sight so astounding, so unusual, so downright erotic, that it is too much for women and children and can only be seen by men of strong constitution."

"What is it?" called someone in the audience.

"It is a woman," Wee Willie began. "Nay! It is twice the woman that any of you have ever experienced, a woman so enticing, so beguiling, so mesmerizing that you won't know where to direct your gaze, and you can see her for a mere few pennies."

The women and children exited the main tent, but most of the men remained behind, paid extra, and filed into the annex behind the curtain.

In the past, the ding had been Tina the Tattooed Woman wearing little more than her all-encompassing tattoos, but I realized that the Harris Twins had not performed as part of the ten-in-one, and that they must be what was hidden behind the curtain.

I asked Tina about it as she helped remove my costume.

"Willie told me about the change this morning. He thought the girls would be a bigger draw, but it sounds like he hasn't perfected the pitch."

"Are they—?"

"They're dressed," she said. "Mostly."

I walked to the annex and peeked through a gap in the tent wall. A dozen men ogled the scantily dressed twins, who were not enjoying the attention.

Wee Willie announced the end of the show. "Thank you for coming, but it's time to move along so we can prepare for the next performance."

Most of the men shuffled out, but one refused to leave. He wanted something more. "I paid my money to see me some flesh," he said as he grabbed at the girls, "and I wanna—"

He didn't finish his sentence. Wee Willie lashed out with his cane, driving it hard into the man's groin and dropping him to his knees. When the man looked up, he found the barrel of Wee Willie's derringer pressed against his forehead.

The girls watched from their specially built seat. I watched through the gap.

Wee Willie cocked the derringer's hammer. "You were saying?"

As the man struggled to his feet and hobbled from the annex, I returned to the cook tent to await the next show. Joyce joined me and we drank watery coffee while discussing our options in low whispers.

"We should leave, Paul," she said. "We should get away from here."

"And go where? And do what?"

"We could join another show," she said. "There are other bearded ladies, but there is no other Human Sea Lion. You could be somebody."

Wee Willie's Hall of Human and Animal Oddities, Wondrous World of Prodigies of Physical Phenomena and Living Human Curiosities had been my only home for the entirety of my adult life, and I could not imagine leaving behind my family, such as they were.

"How would we—?"

Joyce lowered her voice and leaned close to whisper in my ear. "I know the combination to the safe. I was in the dookie wagon this morning and I opened it."

Wee Willie kept the show's cash and date book, which contained the show's route, in a safe in the dookie wagon, and I'd thought no one else had access to them. I hesitated before telling Joyce, "If word ever got out that we'd stolen from Wee Willie, our careers would be over. No one would ever work with us again."

We stared at each other for a moment. Then she lowered her gaze. "A girl can dream, can't she?"

We did four shows that day and planned to do four the next before moving on. That night most of us gathered in the cook tent after dinner, drinking beer, playing cards, and telling tall tales.

Carl, one of the truck drivers, entered the tent and touched Tina's arm to catch her attention. "He wants to see you in his office."

The Tattooed Woman blanched, the natural color draining from her face so that the tattoos which covered most of it appeared as if inked upon a white canvas.

She looked at me, but I looked away.

"I can't," she said. "It's that time of the month."

I could tell from the sound of her voice that Joyce was lying, but Carl couldn't. He shrugged and said, "I'll let him know."

"He'll just find someone else," I said as Carl walked away.

"But it won't be me," she said. "Not tonight. It won't be me."

I looked around, saw Joyce entering the tent, and knew that it also wouldn't be her.

* * * *

In the cook tent the next morning, the Harris twins were not their usual bubbly selves. They sat with Joyce and pushed their food around on their plates without eating.

When Wee Willie strutted into the tent, their reactions to his presence told me everything I needed to know. No one had done anything when he took advantage of the Bearded Lady, the Tattooed Woman, or the Sword Swallower, but this was different. Lettie and Nettie were young girls.

I stood as Wee Willie approached our table. I said, "Leave the twins alone."

"They're mine and I'll do whatever I want." Wee Willie pressed the tip of his cane against my chest. "What are you going to do about it, flipper boy?"

Without thinking, I slapped Wee Willie with my right flipper, knocking him to the ground and sending his top hat rolling away.

Some of the other performers gasped. No one had ever talked back to Wee Willie and remained with the show, and no one had ever knocked him to the ground.

When he drew his Remington Double Derringer, I dove on top of him, pinning him to the ground with my weight. Joyce pried the derringer from Wee Willie's hand and dropped it into her bodice, where it rested in her hairy cleavage.

Wee Willie struggled and spat and swore beneath me, and when I tired of his foul language, I covered his face with my flipper, certain that my time with the show had come to an end. Because Joyce had helped me, I suspected she would also have to leave. I had no idea what to do, so I lay atop Wee Willie until the iron-fisted dwarf quit struggling. When I rolled off of him, I realized why.

The other performers stared at me.

"We have to pack up the show and blow town," I said. I told them we had access to the safe and that we would continue following the route outlined in the date book.

"We can't leave Wee Willie here."

"We'll take him with us," I told them. "We'll make him earn his keep."

After emptying the jar containing the two-headed baby hippo, we stripped Wee Willie, stuffed him inside, and filled the jar with formaldehyde.

* * * *

Two days later, we set up the show in a new town. I took over the talk, using the patter I'd memorized to convince the rubes to shell out hard-earn money to see the Bearded Lady, The Tattooed Lady, the Sword Swallower, the conjoined Harris Twins, and all the rest.

I saved Wee Willie for the ding, using his own spiel as a man "small of stature but all man where it counts" to convince gullible rubes to pay extra to see him in the annex behind the curtain.

Wee Willie turned out to be a bigger attraction dead than he had ever been alive.

Edward D. Hoch Memorial Golden Derringer Award recipient Michael Bracken has written several books, including the private eye novel *All White Girls*, and more than 1,300 short stories, including stories in *Alfred Hitchcock's Mystery Magazine*, *Black Cat Mystery Magazine*, *Ellery Queen's Mystery Magazine*, and *The Best American Mystery Stories*.

EMILY AND ELODIE
BY DARA CARR

As a lady with big knockers, I'm accustomed to a certain level of regard. My water glass, for instance, is always at least half full. And that isn't just a figure of speech.

"More water, Elodie?" asks the cross-eyed boy wearing baggy pants.

He's back at our booth again, dealing water like it's dope, and my cup already runneth over. There's good service and then there's harassment.

"Do I look like I need more fluids?" I ask.

His eyes stray to my chest, as if the ladies are going to answer the question. I point to Emily's nearly empty glass. He blinks, as if seeing for the first time I am sitting across from someone. Giving me a goofy lopsided grin, he fills Emily's glass and splashes some water onto the sugar packets and bottle of hot sauce.

Not that Emily notices. She keeps looking at the door like she's plotting her escape from North Carolina's best buttermilk-batter fried chicken with mashed potatoes and ham gravy. I know it's the best because I've never missed a meal in my life.

Emily, on the other hand, has never eaten a decent meal in her entire existence. She's an itty-bitty thing with skin the bluish shade of skim milk except for a green bruise on her right arm, which she's trying to hide. She looks like the haunted child in a horror movie, the kind levitating at the end of a dim hallway, eyes rolling into the back of her head.

"It's cold in here," Emily says, rubbing her arms. "I think the AC is too high."

She thinks wrong. Being cold all the time is a sign of starvation and demonic possession. Never mind, I pull a silk shawl from my bag and hand it to her.

"Why don't you put this on?"

As she fingers the magenta fabric, she looks like she's about to cry. She gazes at me like I'm the only one who has ever done anything nice for her.

"Go on," I say. "It'll warm you up."

She pulls it around her bony shoulders, disappearing into the luscious fabric.

The water boy is hovering, waiting for my breasts to do something rash. If he insists on hanging about he may as well be put to use.

"What's your name again?" I ask.

He goes all shucks on me, head lolling to the side. "Dwayne."

"Dwayne, I want to introduce you to Emily. She needs some excitement and expensive calories in her life. You look like you could do that for her."

He doesn't look like he remembers his own name most mornings but never mind.

"Hi," Emily says.

Dwayne doesn't respond right away. He pulls a notepad out of his back pocket and jots down something, as if we're placing an order. I shake my head in wonder. Maybe I should help him out, scribble, "Nice to meet you, Emily," on a napkin and press it against my chest.

A moment later, he asks Emily, "How do you like the chicken, miss?"

"It's good, thanks." She gives him a constipated smile. "But I'm not used to food this salty."

Jesus wept.

Dwayne's gaze shifts back to me. He seems to have lost the thread in this veritable tapestry of a conversation. I duck my head, interfering with his sight line to the ladies, and point to my praline bacon waffle with whipped cream and toasted pecans.

"My question to you, Dwayne, is whether there's a man good enough to compete with this waffle. Someone who could give me the same salty sweet ecstasy? You know someone like that?"

His mouth moves but nothing comes out. Just what I thought.

"Scat." I motion him away. "Go spread the joy of water."

Emily stares at the front door like a dog waiting for her master. She's all but whining. There's a neon red sign out front that says "EAT" but that couldn't be her focus. A moment later, I see something worth barking about.

A midnight blue 1970s Firebird drives by slowly. I spotted the car earlier. It must be circling the block. On weekends, it can be tough to park in this part of Durham.

"That car sends me straight into ovulation," I say.

Emily's lips curl then uncurl again. She makes an indistinct noise. I take that as enthusiasm and say, "Isn't it gorgeous?"

She shrinks into her seat. She's trying her best to be invisible. She would be almost undetectable except that the bright pink shawl I lent her sizzles against the cherry red upholstery of our booth.

The Firebird double parks near the door of the cafe. A man gets out. Emily and I track his movement. Finally, we're on the same wavelength. I whistle softly. He is a vision to compete with the praline bacon waffle. He has dark hair, coal eyes, and a firm set to his mouth.

"Perfection in the flesh," I say. "I'll bet he drives fast and knows how to take corners."

Emily stares at her barely touched meal. "He…"

"Probably even does his own transmission work. I love men who are good with their hands."

Emily gazes at the wall, where open shelves show off locally canned jams, sauces, and relishes. She seems to be outdone by this man's grandeur.

She manages to say, "He, uh…"

"Is right in time for dessert. I could eat him whole."

Truth is, he looks a little cranky at the moment. He stands outside the door to the cafe, arms crossed. But cranky is fixable, way better than cheap, and can be managed with the right lighting.

"He's my husband," Emily says.

I nearly choke on my tongue. "You're kidding."

This flyspeck, this broken toy, this haunted child with the bluish white skin is married? Sure enough, if I squint hard, I can see the tiny doll's ring on her finger.

"You little devil!" I say. "You've got him giving you door-to-door service?"

She's fishing around in her canvas tote bag. "I have to leave."

Before I know it, my finger is wagging. "We're not done yet. You've barely eaten anything. He needs to wait. It's good for men to wait for what they want."

She pulls out a sandwich baggie with some crumpled bills in it. No kidding, this is her wallet. I should adopt her for thirty dollars a month. She could get a new wallet plus buy the occasional ice cream sundae.

"Sorry," she says.

"Only Jesus Christ in the flesh can interrupt a meal this good."

"This is my fault. I gave him the wrong time." She gives me a pleading look. "We've got a lot to do today. You understand, right?"

"No, I don't understand. I don't go anywhere unless I'm good and ready."

"Really?" Her eyes widen.

"Really."

She extracts a few bills and puts them on the table. I sweep them back up and stuff them into her pathetic baggie.

"Your money isn't good today. This is my treat. I invited you."

She presses her lips together. "I can't let you pay, not when I'm the one ruining our meal."

"Don't feel bad about it being my money. You can thank Randall for the meal."

"Randall?" She stows the money back in her tote bag.

"My late great husband, who had the foresight to purchase excellent life insurance before he passed away."

Foresight might be a bit of an exaggeration, but never mind.

I wave at her hubby, standing guard at the door. He smolders in my direction. Emily dashes past two rows of wooden tables and skitters out the door. She jumps into the Firebird. The hubby follows behind, strolling, taking time to not only smell the coffee but the roses as well. This man needs to go back for more training.

The waiter appears, and I ask him to box up Emily's food for me to take home.

A moment later, Dwayne is back. "More water?"

I'm about to tell him where to go when I see my glass is almost empty. Someone must have turned up the heat in here.

"Thank you, sweetheart." I smile up at him. "I thought you'd never ask."

Emily sits in the glorious Firebird staring straight ahead. She's got my shawl wrapped around her like a hug. This woman needs help.

* * * *

Emily's house is grand, which is what you'd expect from a horror movie child. It's a white colonial with black shutters and two urns of yellow mums flanking the front door. To the side of the house is a three-car garage. The mister loves his cars.

I ring the bell, and a second later Emily appears. We're supposed to go speed walking today. She's dressed to scrub the toilet. She's wearing stained beige capris, cheap tennis shoes, and a faded t-shirt. Her bra has no support.

If she's possessed, it's by the wrong type of spirit. I never go speed walking, but I know how to dress for the occasion: purple spandex top, black bottoms with a matching purple stripe, and a metallic silver backpack.

Emily turns, and I see a big bruise like an apple juice stain on the back of her left calf. She probably hasn't noticed it yet, that's why she's not wearing full-length pants.

She starts walking to the left, going the wrong way. Why am I not surprised?

"Let's go the other way." I point behind us, the direction that will eventually lead to a bakery I want to visit.

Emily's mouth puckers. "That's not the way I usually go."

"Does the way you go lead to a bakery that sells brown sugar cardamom cake?"

Her preteen chest rises and falls. "We're supposed to be exercising."

"I need incentives for peak performance."

"What's the point of speed walking to a bakery?" Even as she asks the question, she turns around, rerouting.

"What's the point of walking fast to get nowhere?"

She starts walking, and fast. "Cardiovascular benefits."

"I think it's bad for your heart to do anything you don't want to do."

Her arms are swinging hard. I wouldn't be surprised if a bone or two fell off her from the exertion.

"You don't do anything you don't want to do?" Emily asks.

"Correct."

"Housework?"

"Nope."

"Grocery shopping?"

I laugh. "I don't even water my own plants. I pay a man in my building to take care of the garden on my terrace."

"Is there anything you do that you don't want to?"

I pretend to think about it as we pass a magnificent magnolia tree. "I read financial statements."

These days, I have leisure class problems.

She stares straight ahead. "You're lucky."

Like most fortunate people, the concept of luck makes me nervous.

"Believe me, I haven't always had it this good. I had to fight hard for my way of life. I suffered for a long time."

We walk quietly for a while, except for my huffing. Before us stretches an eternity of stately, well-maintained homes. Where is that bakery?

"This a nice quiet area," Emily says. "Great for families."

Like those are good things. Being well-endowed, two of the words I fear most are 'maternal' and 'matronly.' And those are pluses in this community.

"I love to be in the middle of the city, surrounded by hustle and bustle."

Emily picks up the pace. "I like the sound of birds."

"Birds wake up too early in the morning for my taste. But I do like the cry of the wild, so long as it's coming from my bedroom."

"Oh, Elodie." She laughs through closed lips.

Thankfully, this slows her down a little. Up ahead, thank the stars, I spot the blue and yellow façade of the bakery.

"What do you like to do in your spare time?" I ask.

She walks a little faster. I try to keep pace but I'm testing the structural limits of spandex, not to mention my well-marbled heart.

"I don't know." She gives it a think and says, "We go to car shows."

"My darling late husband Randall loved cars. That's what killed him in the end."

Emily gives me a sharp look. "It sounds like our husbands would have had a lot in common."

"You're not a car nut, are you?"

"No."

"What kind of nut are you then?"

She gives me a sly grin. "I like to go to Dimsy's Cafe and eat the praline bacon waffle."

I laugh. "That's me. We're talking about you."

She turns her attention to her speed walking. "I don't know."

"Rock climbing?" I ask.

She laughs. "No way."

"You've got the figure for it. How about gardening?"

"I've got a black thumb. I kill everything."

"That doesn't stop me."

"I'm taking kickboxing," she says.

It's my turn to laugh. "You sparring with people?"

"Not yet, we're still learning how to kick."

"How long before you get to the boxing part?"

"I'm not sure."

"Maybe you should get yourself a German Shepherd. That's a good, loyal animal. It'll rip the intestines out of your enemies."

"I've got allergies."

Of course she does. "You want to protect yourself, get a gun."

She glances at me. "Or a heavy car?"

I give her a hard stare. Her smile flees. She looks like she's about to run back inside herself and hide. I let the comment pass.

"Better yet, forget speed walking," I say. "Learn how to run."

* * * *

As we approach Emily's house, her husband comes out onto the front steps, arms crossed against his chest. He's wearing a sour expression, as if Emily is late for something. This man is a pill.

Mustering up some energy from the last of my cardamom cake reserves, I breathe deep and call out to him. "Hello there."

I straighten up, letting the spandex work its magic with my figure. He looks about as friendly as a security guard. Any friendlier and he might pull a gun on me.

"We broke speed walking records today," I say. "Aren't you going to congratulate us?"

The arms unfold. The legs take him down the steps and onto the front walk. Digging deep, he even offers a hand when we're introduced. His name is Mike.

"She loves your car," Emily says.

That's about as far as we get before Emily goes into haunted child mode, all averted gazes and forehead sweat. Her head swivels around.

"Where did you park, Elodie?" she asks.

I pull out my cell phone. "I didn't. I like to ride in cars, not drive them. I'll call a ride service. A driver will be here in a few minutes."

Emily kneads her hands. She turns to her husband, "Maybe you…"

Mike says, "I'll drive you home."

I angle my head at him. "No, I don't want to be a bother."

Mike smiles. Amazing his face doesn't crack with the effort.

"It's no bother," he replies. "I'm happy to take you home."

He walks over to the Firebird and opens the front passenger side door.

"Such a gentleman," I say, my voice sticky with brown butter and pralines.

I turn, looking for Emily, and catch the back of her, heading through the door of the house.

"Ta, Emily," I call out.

I slide into the car and run my hands over the white upholstery. Inside, it smells like leather and engine oil. Oh my.

He gets into the car, and we drive off, toward downtown.

"You like cars?" he says.

"Some cars," I reply. "Is this a regular Firebird or a Super Duty model?"

I assume it's a regular Firebird, but I can be a bit of a show-off with car trivia. It's something that irritated me about my late husband, and here I am doing the same thing, proof that he was as infectious as the pox.

Mike, however, doesn't seem to think I was showing off. He appears to be in awe, or what passes for that in a man of few words.

"Good eye," he says.

"Seriously?" I squeal a little. "This is a Super Duty?"

He nods, pressing his lips together, trying not to beam, trying not to show his excitement.

"The one with the racing engine in the street car?" I ask.

"Yes."

This was the fastest street-legal car of its time. I'm like one of those women on a game show, bobbing with excitement.

"An engine that weighs at least 650 pounds?" I can't help myself.

"Yes." The iceman melts.

"A real monster under the hood," I say.

"Uh huh," he replies.

"I'm in love."

What I especially love is that my darling late Randall, roasting in hell, must be screaming his lungs out. Here I am, riding in a car he lusted after much of his life but never possessed. The car costs at least a hundred thousand dollars, if you can even find one to buy. Pontiac produced these cars for only two years, in 1973 and 1974.

"How do you know about Super Duty Firebirds?"

"My late husband was a car nut. He used to dream about owning a Super Duty."

He gives me a sidelong glance. "Married to you, that's what he dreamed about?"

I feel a rumble from under the hood. "I'm afraid so."

"You like the food at Dimsy's?"

"Love it," I say. "I'm a regular."

"Every weekend?"

"Plus Fridays."

"That's your beauty secret."

"It makes me happy." I smile. "Only a few things can make me happier."

"You hungry right now?"

I give him a ravenous look. "No."

We drive for a while in silence. I like that he can keep quiet. Eventually we reach my place.

"Nice," he says, peering up at my condo building, a former tobacco factory made into a glamorous lady lair with floor-to-ceiling windows.

"It certainly is," I reply, wondering how hard he's going to try.

"I hope I'll get to see you again," he says.

As I slide out of the car, I laugh, letting him know I'm unimpressed, and say, "*That* sounds like a plan."

* * * *

Late morning on Friday, I am at Dimsy's, tucking into crispy fried catfish with a side of creamy fennel slaw. Sam, the manager, appears, loitering overhead like freeway smog. Balls. And just when the meal was going so well.

"Hi, handsome," I say.

"Where's your new friend? You scare her away already?"

"What new friend?"

"Skinny blond lady. The one you were dining with last week."

"She's married."

"Not for long, not with you around." He grins, pleased with his dig, and I get to enjoy the smell of burnt coffee on his breath.

"For your information, I'm trying to help her."

"Help her." His shoulders start shaking. The mirth then migrates to his gut, which quivers, before it shoots out his flabby mouth. He brays with laughter, shaking hard.

"Be careful you don't wet yourself. At a certain age, the body can't take much abuse."

He pats my shoulder. "Neither of us is getting any younger, Elodie."

"Speak for yourself."

"About this new friend, you're going to help her do what? Destroy her life?"

"I'm introducing her to the finer things in life, like the food here."

"Did she actually taste any of the food you're helping her enjoy, or did you eat it all?"

I stare at the catfish. "Maybe you should go back to selling insurance."

His head angles dangerously. "What did you say?"

"Where's that nice water boy?"

Sam points at my glass. "It's completely full, Elodie."

"Not for long." I give him a meaningful look. "Anyway, I like talking to that water boy. What's his name again?"

"Dwayne." All three of Sam's chins quiver with disapproval. "You handle that young man with care. He looks normal enough, but he's recovering from a serious brain injury."

"One part of his brain still seems to be working fine. Or maybe that's only muscle memory."

"Be nice, Elodie."

Sam is a sucker for strays and sorry tales of woe.

"You sure he should be with customers?" I ask.

"You want him off the floor?"

"I want your assessment."

"He's fine. This job is helping him. His doctor says social stimulation is good for his recovery."

"You don't say." *Social stimulation.* I gaze up at the pressed tin ceiling and smile.

"On the other hand, he doesn't always remember when he's supposed to be working. He still has to write a lot down. But he's getting better and better."

"Good," I say, deciding I don't have the energy to burst this particular bubble.

"Enough about Dwayne," Sam says. "How did you and your skinny blond married friend meet?"

"At a carry-out place. They got our names mixed up and gave me her lunch by mistake."

Samuel raises his caterpillar eyebrows. "Didn't take you long to figure that out, did it."

I smile. "The second I lifted that brown paper bag I knew something was terribly wrong."

"Air salad with a side of nothing?" He throws his head back and laughs. "That's how you found out she was dying for a good meal?"

"That's when I promised to treat her at Dimsy's. How could I not help this poor starving woman?"

He gives me a beatific smile. I take a deep breath, bracing myself. Not this again.

"I miss you, Elodie," he says.

"We've been through this before, sweetheart."

Someone from the kitchen flags Sam down. With one last soulful look, he takes off. Relieved, I drink some water.

Moments later, Dwayne stands before me, transfixed.

"Honey," I say. "I'm finished. You can go water someone else."

He stares at the ladies. "Done?"

"Go on, go see who else needs fluids."

After another goggle, he mopes away, in search of other forms of social stimulation.

I pick up my check. As I'm squinting at the numbers, I sense someone hovering nearby. I look up and find Emily's husband is gazing at me like it's Christmas morning.

"What a wonderful surprise," I say.

"I was hoping I'd run into you."

He smells like soap and his fingernails are scrubbed clean, which is a big deal for a car nut. He isn't lying about hoping to see me. He's prepared.

I give him an apologetic look. "I'm getting ready to leave."

"Perfect," he says, gesturing to the check. "May I get that for you?"

I pause a beat. "Thank you, that's awfully kind."

No one would believe he has a starving wife at home.

He drops a twenty-dollar bill on the table. I like that he pays in cash.

"I thought you might want another ride in the Firebird," he says.

I gaze out the plate glass window, where the car is parked near the door. "That's a beautiful car."

"And you're a beautiful lady."

"Uh huh."

"Plus, I thought you might want dessert."

"I really shouldn't," I say. "They feed me so well here."

He gazes at me, eyebrows raised expectantly.

"But I never turn down dessert," I say.

* * * *

We go to a romantic dessert place. It has a green and white banner and fairy lights strung across a cobblestone courtyard. We sit near a small fountain, which is surrounded by red flowers. A waiter gives us menus.

Mike asks, "What do you do for a living?"

I glance at the menu and say, "Nothing." My heart thumps when I see they've got at least ten flavors of gelato.

"Guess what I do for a living," he says.

I stare at him. He can't seriously think I care what he does for a living, especially not with a selection of gelato on my mind.

He grins and says, "I sell refrigerator magnets."

"Really." He knows how to spoil the mood.

"No."

After pondering what toasted marshmallow might taste like, I order tiramisu gelato. Mike goes traditional with stracciatella.

After we order, he asks, "You don't have a job?"

I sigh. He's no conversationalist.

"I used to work at a salon before my husband died."

"Did you like working there?"

I didn't like it, not at all. It was dirty, smelly, punishing work. But I surprise myself by saying, "I enjoyed making people feel better. Some women would come in worn out by their jobs, their kids, their lives. They'd leave glowing, looking like different people."

"I also like to leave people glowing."

The gelatos arrive. I hate to leave that last hot comment sizzle into nothing, but I can't multitask when it comes to dessert.

After the first mouthful, I realize the tiramisu was a good choice. Is that coffee liqueur among the mascarpone, vanilla bean, and cocoa? Or did they use both espresso powder and liqueur?

A few minutes later, Mike says, "You're done."

He's still got half his gelato left. He and Emily share some bad habits.

"When something is delicious, I can't help myself," I say.

"I'm a slow eater. Why don't you help me?"

A man who can't finish his gelato is my kind of date.

He spoons his stracciatella and feeds it to me. Oh my.

After we finish, we get back into the Firebird. We drive about a block when he tells me he'd like to take me to his rental garage. This does nothing for my mood.

"Garage?" I ask, drawing the word out, letting him know what I think.

"Trust me," he says.

It's my policy to never trust anyone unless at gunpoint. I make a low, humming noise.

He says, "If you don't like it we'll leave right away."

Fifteen minutes later, I follow him inside the garage, a nondescript beige brick building. The sight of a seven hundred fifty model BMW on car jacks makes my skin crawl. On the bright side, you could scream bloody murder in this place and no one would hear you.

"You're losing me," I say.

He smiles. "I've got a secret."

I like secrets, having plenty myself. But I don't let him off the hook.

"This better be good," I say.

He leads me into a side room, which has a large black leather couch and a flat-screen TV and, best of all, champagne chilling in a bucket. He closes the door, and voila, the garage disappears. Within seconds, he's got a remote in his hand, and the sound of jazz fills the room.

I eye the champagne. "Expecting someone?"

"Hoping. Desperately hoping."

I sit down on the sofa. "Pour me a glass, and let's hope this couch can withstand some serious abuse."

Two months later

It is almost noon on Friday, and I am finished with my shrimp and grits. Dwayne, the giver of water, has paid multiple visits to my table, each time pausing for some social stimulation. The check awaits my attention.

I glance at the front door. Emily jogs by the cafe. She does this every so often, always at the same time: right before her husband comes calling for me. Maybe it's my imagination but she looks good, stronger and more life-like.

I'm not sure why she jogs in this area. She never looks or comes inside the cafe. But she must know I'm here. She also must know her husband comes here. He's been doing that for a while now. We've got a pattern, or at least I thought we did. I check the time on my cell-phone. He's late.

Sam comes to my table. His instincts for trouble are impeccable. "Waiting for someone?" he asks.

"My personal trainer."

"He's got you trained alright," he says.

I let my head loll back on my neck. "You've got that wrong."

"He's been turning up later and later. He doesn't seem to be picking up the check anymore, either."

"Don't you have a job to do?"

"You're in love." He whistles softly. "You two have been carrying on for weeks now, must be a record for you."

"It's not like that." Mike is only good for two things, and I have the sense to know it.

Sam does a mock shiver. "I don't want to be here the day that man doesn't show up. In fact, I don't want to be within five hundred miles of you that day."

"Enough."

He lets a few beats pass. "You look like you could use a friend."

"I'm fine, Sam. But it's kind of you to be concerned."

On cue, Dwayne arrives. "More water, Elodie?"

I hold my head in my hands.

Sam puts a meaty arm around Dwayne's shoulder. "Miss Elodie is fine. She's getting ready to leave."

"Don't go," Dwayne says to my breasts.

"Dwayne, you know what day this is?" Sam asks, his voice soft.

"Friday."

Sam offers up a small smile. "And what does that mean?"

Dwayne looks at me. That's not going to cut it for a reply, at least not for Sam.

Sam sighs and says, "You don't work on Fridays."

Dwayne's baby pink lips form a circle. He takes the notepad from his back pocket and writes in it.

"Sorry, Sam. I'll go now."

We watch as Dwayne ambles out the door.

I turn to Sam. "You're right. He's getting better and better."

"Whatever happened to that skinny blond woman, your friend?" he asks.

"Nothing," I say.

"She got all the help she needed from you and then some."

"Some people are beyond help," I say.

His expression turns to mush. "No one is beyond help, and you should know that."

"She'll thank me," I say. "It's going to take about ten years. But it will happen."

"Ten years, huh. That's some help you must have given her. Maybe you need to find a new hobby, like Zumba or yoga."

This gives me an idea. "I haven't been to the racetrack in ages. I used to love to go."

"There's a new Zumba class at my church. You'll meet some nice people there."

"Nothing wrong with the people at the speedway."

He laughs. "You going to meet a nice man at the track?"

"I'm done with nice."

"You've got to try it first."

I arch an eyebrow at him. "You sustain a brain injury or something?"

He blushes. "You've got to try it *again* sometime."

"The track is a perfect place for meeting men." I smile. "Nothing wrong with a fool and his money."

Sam laughs. "Speaking of which, your personal trainer is here."

Mike stands near the front door, arms crossed, waiting for me.

* * * *

The next day, on Saturday, I sit at my corner booth at Dimsy's, pondering the menu. Emily, wearing a hat and sunglasses, appears out of nowhere and sits across from me. She acts as though nothing has happened. Even though I smell sulfur, I play along.

"You want to split a side of smoked bacon?" I ask.

She shakes her head. "Too salty for my taste."

The waiter arrives. Emily orders huevos rancheros to go. I order the bananas foster french toast to stay.

Now that I know she's not planning to linger, I ask, "How's the kickboxing?"

"I don't do that any longer." She gives me an impish grin.

"Things are going well?"

"Couldn't be better," she says.

Indeed, her skin doesn't give off an eerie pale blue glow any longer. Still, I wonder if she's being sarcastic. She doesn't seem to be, but I've been known to miss that sort of thing on occasion.

"I understand why you may be angry," I say.

She gives me a blank look.

"Your husband is just like my darling late Randall. Can't live with him, can't live with him."

"Mike is dead."

I pick my jaw off the floor. "What?"

"A car fell on him while he was working on it. It had a problem with the steering linkage. The tires were off, and he was under the heaviest part of the car when the jack stands failed."

The world shifts under me. I take a long drink of water. "That's what happened to Randall, my husband. A car fell on him."

"I know. I Googled it."

"You shouldn't have done that," I say. "The police are going to think you did it. Things like that don't happen twice by chance."

"I Googled it at one of the computers at the library downtown."

My flesh is starting to prickle. I'm still processing when I say, "The police are going to know we're friends."

She folds her hands. "They're going to know that you and my late husband were friends. They're going to know that you two were together every Friday afternoon. And that's approximately when he was sent to his maker, thanks to the bad jack stands."

"Yesterday?" I say, still trying to cut through haze.

"Indeed," she replies. "The police are also going to discover the jack stands had the same issues as the ones your late husband used."

Not only is her color good, she doesn't seem cold any longer. It's my turn to feel a chill in the air.

"My shawl."

She gives me a wincing smile. "I'm afraid the police found it in the garage. They consider it evidence."

My mind is whirring. "Why would I hurt your husband?"

"He refused to leave me for you."

"I didn't want him to leave you. It was almost over between us."

She crosses her arms against her chest, looking smug. "He was about to dump you. The same way Randall was about to dump you just before he met his untimely end. You have anger management issues."

Isn't Google a bitch.

I stare at the pale yellow wall, my mind whirring. "They'll realize you wanted revenge on him."

"They know we've been in counseling and were planning to renew our vows next month in Valle Crucis." She lifts a hand in the air, showing off a big adult diamond ring.

The waiter arrives with Emily's food in a carryout box. She hands him a twenty and tells him to keep the change. She even knows to pay cash, like her husband did.

I give the waiter a shrug. "You can box my order up as well. I can't stay."

He disappears with my food.

Emily smiles. "I've got to run. Ta, Elodie."

She's gone in a blink. Heat is rising from my body in waves, and I need a minute to get my bearings. I drink some water.

I should run. The problem is I finally have my life exactly the way I want it. But no one will believe me. They'll believe the poor, put-upon wife.

I dip a napkin into the water and mop my forehead. I have the money to disappear. The problem with running is that once you start you never stop.

"More water, Elodie?" Dwayne asks.

I'm about to shoo him away. But then I see my water glass could use replenishment. I smile up at him. He's growing on me, in a sort of convenient way.

"Thank you for a lovely time yesterday afternoon," I say.

He scrunches his brows. "Yesterday?"

"You don't remember." I pout.

Frowning, he pulls the notepad from his back pocket. He quickly pages through it.

"I went to the park Friday afternoon," he says. "You weren't with me."

I hold my hand out. "Give me that."

He takes a step backward, a stricken expression on his baby face. "I can't."

"I'm not going to steal it."

"It's my life," he says, his lips quivering.

"Sweetheart, I promise I'll be careful," I say. "And give me your pen too."

He reluctantly hands them over to me. I flip through the notepad until I find Friday's notes. Copying his handwriting, I make a few entries on the page.

When I'm done, he studies what I wrote. "We were at the park together on Friday afternoon. After that, we went to your place."

"That's right."

He stares at my chest. "We had a nice time?"

"A wonderful time." I smile. "You were great."

He gives me a goofy, lopsided grin. "I was great?"

"Yes, you were," I reply. "Now shoo, go spread the joy of water."

✗

Maryland writer Dara Carr is the author of the novel, *Angela Cray Gets Real*, a Freddie Award finalist. Her short fiction has appeared in *Alfred Hitchcock's Mystery Magazine*, *Ellery Queen's Mystery Magazine*, and *Shotgun Honey*. You can find her and the occasional tumbleweed at www.daracarr.com.

PARTNERS IN CRIME
TRACY FALENWOLFE

Clyde Eggars kicked his mark in the ribs. His last mark. A cloud of dust rose up and hung in front of his Caddy's headlights. "Get his feet."

Travis, the young gun who was supposed to be helping on this job, pitched forward from the waist and squinted at the heap that used to be Marshall Pittman. "Are you sure he's dead?"

Clyde smoothed his tie and tucked the end of it into his pants. If Pittman wasn't dead, he would be when they tossed him off the pier. Who was Travis to question him, anyway? The kid was there to watch and learn. Not to quiz.

"See if he's breathing if you're not sure," Clyde said. A sense of nostalgia overwhelmed him as he reamed the kid. It was sweet, like the Sen-Sen he used to carry in the early days of his career. He'd picked up the habit from Benny, the guy who'd shown him the ropes.

Clyde and Benny'd had their differences. Benny liked animals and the outdoors. Several of his jobs had gone down in history as hunting accidents. One of Benny's favorite ways to get someone to talk was to administer repeated snake bites. Benny had even named the damn snake he used, like it was a pet. Called it Fluffy, which was demented now that Clyde thought about it.

Clyde hated animals, and bugs, and anything that lived outdoors, generally, but he respected Benny so he'd learned from him.

Clyde liked to think that respect had been mutual. Once, back in the day, Sid had taken his key players on a deep-sea fishing trip. Benny noticed Clyde was the only one who wouldn't handle the fish and had covered for him. Of course, no one was paying any attention to what Clyde was or wasn't doing after one of the guys ended up as bait and the reason for the fishing trip became clear. Now Clyde was the one trying to be a good mentor like Benny had been to him, but the wisdom he was trying to impart fell on deaf ears.

Travis wiped the back of his sweaty hand across his mouth. "*You* see if he's breathing."

Smartass. Maybe Clyde shouldn't bother trying so hard. The kid probably didn't deserve anybody's wisdom, anyway.

"You should have let me shoot him," Clyde said. He'd been looking forward to this one last hit. The kid had taken it away from him when he'd bounced Pittman off the fender and screwed up the plan.

Why had Pittman gotten out of his car like that, anyway?

Whatever the reason, Clyde never should have let Travis drive. He'd gotten too close to Pittman, and they'd been made. Still, Clyde had been about to take a shot from the car, until Travis panicked and swerved.

"Whatever," Travis said. "It's done, right?"

These young kids had no pride. Clyde waved his hand toward the back of his Caddy. "Open the trunk and then come get his feet." They were close enough to the marsh that the rotten egg smell seeped in through his nostrils and hung at the back of his throat. Some things about the job he wouldn't miss.

"I thought you had the keys," Travis mumbled. "Why can't you open the trunk?" Even though it was dark, Clyde could see the disinterested look on Travis's face. No way the kid was right for this job. He had no respect for it. He couldn't even dress the part.

Like Benny before him, Clyde always wore a suit. He shaved every day and wore cologne and kept his hands manicured. Travis wore baggy jeans and a sweatshirt. He shaved his head, and had a tattoo on his neck, and couldn't look away from his phone for longer than twenty seconds at a time.

Even still, he might have saved their asses on this job. Clyde looked at the stiff on the ground.

"Why did you get out of the car like that?"

Travis looked up. Barely. "You say something, Hoss?"

"I said open the door and pop the trunk if you don't have the keys on you."

Pittman shouldn't have gotten out of his car, not where they were in the middle of nowhere. But something wasn't right about this whole job, now that Clyde thought about it. His last hit ever, and Sid hadn't even assigned it himself? Sid Jr. had called Clyde to the penthouse to give him the details. Sure, Jr. was working his way up the ranks, but Clyde deserved Sid's respect one last time, didn't he?

The bugs were so loud it sounded like the trees were alive. It made Clyde's skin crawl. He twitched and lifted his shoulder to shoo a mosquito that landed on his neck. He hated August. He should have retired in May, before the humidity.

Travis popped the trunk and lifted his end of the dead weight. "So how many times you done this?"

Clyde dumped Pittman in the trunk and slammed it. "None of your business."

Travis wiped his hands on his pants and went back to texting.

May had been unseasonably cool. Clyde tried to quit then, right after he found out about the cancer, but the boss had promised him a nice retirement if he helped train his replacement. He knew Travis was Sid's friggin' nephew, but seriously, this guy as a hitter? Clyde didn't even trust him to drive. Not anymore. "Give me the keys."

"I told ya, I don't have 'em." Travis felt all of his pockets. In the glow of the taillights he looked like he was molesting himself.

Clyde counted to three. "Maybe you stuck them under the mat."

"Maybe."

"Well?"

"Well what?"

"Well go look under the mat!"

"I locked the door after I popped the trunk." Travis shuffled his weight from one foot to the other while his thumb worked like mad on his phone. "Sorry, man, it's a habit. Can't we just leave him here?"

"No." Clyde saw his own hand moving, but it was too late to stop himself.

"Owwch." Travis jumped back and juggled his phone like a hot potato. He finally caught it before it hit the ground. "You smacked me!"

The kid needed a smack. Needed to learn how to take one, needed to learn how to mete one out. "Just be glad I didn't shoot you." Three more weeks. Clyde had to get through three more weeks with Travis, then it was off to the Riviera. He wasn't going to waste his retirement on surgeries and radiation and chemo. He was going to live in luxury.

Travis rubbed his temple. "My uncle's gonna hear about this," he mumbled under his breath.

You bet he is, kid. On Clyde's first job, back in the day, he'd been so jacked up he could barely sit still. But he pulled himself together enough to look into the rat's eyes and let him know that what he had coming was compliments of Sidney Frickin' Marchese, and that it was gonna hurt, and that Clyde was the one who was gonna make sure of it.

This kid wasn't interested in any of that. Maybe the boss was punishing Clyde for even bringing up retirement. Or maybe this was something else entirely.

"Sid Jr.is your cousin, right?"

Travis snorted. "So?"

"So you two get along?"

"We used to."

"You used to." Clyde wanted to smack the kid again. "But you don't anymore? What happened?"

"A girl," Travis said. "My girl now. But Sid Jr. was into her first."

Clyde hung his head. "Get a rock."

"Yeah, hold on." The kid had his nose in his phone again.

"Get a rock." Clyde pulled out his pistol and pointed it at Travis. He didn't bother with the counting this time.

"Okay, man." Travis put his hands up. "Don't shoot. I'll get you a rock. Just put that thing away. Put it away and I won't even tell my uncle."

Clyde snorted. Tell his uncle what? That he was a lazy-assed, snot-nosed brat who had no real interest in the family business? At the rate this kid was going Sid would probably consider it a favor if Clyde removed him from the payroll. "I'll put it away as soon as you get a rock and break the window."

"Okay." Travis shuffled backwards slowly. The headlights were behind him, so with every step he took he looked more like a dark, faceless silhouette with an all-over halo. Dust motes rose up from his feet and hovered waist-high, shimmering.

"Turn around and watch where you're walking," Clyde said, squinting at the light. "I ain't gonna shoot you in the back."

"You sure?"

"Kid, I ain't the one you should be afraid of," Clyde said. "Can't you see we've been set up?"

"No way. My uncle wouldn't do that to me."

"Yeah, well, I'm betting your cousin would. I'm also betting we've got about five minutes or less before the cops show up. They'll be looking for us up where we were supposed to be. Pittman getting out of the car probably bought us a few minutes. Now let's go."

"Sid Jr.? He set us up? How? Why, man?"

"Why? Because you're screwing his girl, that's why. How doesn't matter. We've gotta make tracks. Let's go."

It all made sense now. Sid probably didn't even know Pittman. Jr. had set up the hit in order to take his cousin out, and now Clyde was going to get caught in the crossfire. Jr. probably thought it didn't matter anyway since Clyde was on his way out. He was no good to the family anymore. No threat either.

Unless he turned state's evidence.

Why would Jr. take that risk? Short answer: He wouldn't. That meant it wouldn't be the cops headed their way. Jr. himself was coming to take Travis out. He'd have to kill Clyde too, if that were the case, because he wouldn't want to chance Clyde going to Sid Sr.

Senior had a long-standing rule against personal vendettas. Business was business, he always said. "Do what needs to be done and only what needs to be done and keep your personal feelings out of it."

Either way, Clyde was on the lousy end of this deal.

"We're in a mess," Clyde said. "We're sitting ducks."

A long, slow, guttural howl made all the hair on his arms stand up. He looked at Travis. "Did you hear that?"

"Yeah, man." Travis wiped the back of his hand across his mouth again. The motion cut a swath through the ring of dust surrounding him. "I heard it." He slipped his phone into his pocket. "What do you think it was?"

"I dunno." Clyde looked from side to side but couldn't see more than a couple of feet in either direction. "Maybe a coyote or something. Maybe he smells the dead meat in the trunk." He slapped at another mosquito, or maybe it was a black fly this time. Whatever it was, it buzzed. "I hate the friggin' outdoors."

"Look." Travis still had his hands up, but he was thrusting his chin toward the ground. "There at my feet. I'm gonna pick up that rock, okay? Don't shoot."

"Just do it."

"Fine."

The kid crouched down.

"Come on, hurry up." Clyde motioned with his gun.

Travis rose and gave the window a half-hearted tap. "It's not breaking."

"Hit it harder."

"I'm hitting it as hard as I can."

Clyde squeezed off a round, and Travis crumpled like he'd taken one to the chest. "Jeez!" He clamped his hands to his head. "You can warn a guy when you're gonna do that right next to him."

The howl came again. Followed by an answering howl. Whatever was out there, it sounded like there was a pack of them.

Travis looked at Clyde with big stupid doe eyes. "It's funny the gunshot didn't scare off the coyote, isn't it?"

"I don't know." Clyde didn't want to think about it anymore. "Just get the keys." His ears were ringing now, so if a fly buzzed around him he wouldn't be able to hear it. He wouldn't know it was there until he felt it bite into his flesh and start sucking his blood.

"I think it's getting closer," Travis said.

"Yeah, yeah." Clyde felt flies crawling all over him. "Keys. Now."

Travis looked under the mat. "They're not here."

"Then hotwire it."

"I don't know how."

Clyde swatted the air with his gun. "Look it up on your goddamn phone."

"You scared?" Travis's voice quivered.

"No." Clyde strained to see beyond the tree line. "But I'm thinking maybe it's a bear out there and not a coyote." He could feel eyes on him. Smell the musk of something getting close. Watching. Waiting to pounce.

The kid tapped and scrolled. His lips moved as he read. "I need a screwdriver." He looked up at Clyde. "Or a knife."

Clyde had a switchblade in his boot, but he wasn't giving it to the kid. They didn't have time for that. "Forget it," Clyde said. "Just pop the trunk again. We need to get out of here."

"Uhhh…" Travis was sweating bullets. Clyde could smell it even over the marsh.

"Don't worry, I ain't gonna shoot you." The ringing in Clyde's ears faded and he could hear the bugs again. He put his gun back in his shoulder rig.

"Then why do I gotta pop the trunk?"

"To get Pittman's keys. We'll take his car. But we gotta move now."

"I ain't stickin' my hand in no dead guy's pockets."

Clyde saw flies swarming in the starburst of light around the kid's head. He felt itchy all over. "Yes you are."

"Why me?"

The howl came again. It sounded closer. Hungrier. Clyde glanced back at the trees. He could have sworn he saw movement. "You want to get eaten by a bear?"

Travis shook his head violently. The flies scattered. "Seriously. How many times you done this. Like ten? Twelve?"

Twelve? What a pisher. "A hundred and sixty-two. And I'm not going down on my last job. Now pop the trunk."

Travis did. He seemed interested for the first time all night. "That's a lot, man. How many cops? Two? Three?"

"Nine."

Travis whistled. He came to the back of the car as the trunk lid rose up slowly. "That was you last week, wasn't it? That cop on South Street wasn't a drive by. It was you."

"Yeah, that was me." Clyde looked in the trunk at the stiff. "See. No boogeyman. Just a dead guy. Now grab his keys already and let's get moving before your cousin—"

A noise exploded inside Clyde's head. He stumbled backwards and fell on his ass before he even realized Pittman had shot him. Clyde raised his gun to shoot back, but Travis kicked it out of his hand.

Pittman was out of the trunk now, and obviously not dead. He and Travis stood hip to hip, and both of them had guns trained on Clyde.

"You okay, partner?" Travis said.

Partner?

"Just dandy," Pittman said. "Glad you weren't number ten."

"Same goes. You flew off that bumper like a deer. I was worried."

"Nah. It went just like we practiced."

Travis gave Pittman a sideways glance. "Not *just* the way. You got a little carried away with the animal noises, don't you think?"

Pittman shrugged. "I was getting bored in there." A big gold shield flashed at his hip. "Besides, you spent all that time rigging the speakers, so I figured I might as well use them, right? Make sure you got your money's worth." He pressed a button on his phone and the howling started again. "Make sure we call enough coyotes in. That's some mating call they have, isn't it?"

"Remind me to put you in for a promotion," Travis said.

"You're a cop?" Blood pumped from Clyde's wound. "You're both cops?"

Travis winked at him. "You catch on fast, Clyde."

Clyde's vision was cutting in and out. "But you're Sid's nephew."

"Yeah." Travis smiled. He didn't look like a kid anymore. "I'm that, too."

Clyde heard a rustling in the woods. His whole body went cold. "I'll testify. Take me in. I'll rat out anyone, just don't leave me here."

"Oh, you won't live long enough to testify," Travis said. "Once we dump you in the woods the coyotes will eat what's left of your guts. Hopefully you'll be dead first." He leaned in close. "Oh, ah, just in case you're confused from losing all that blood, this is me telling you what you've got coming. Just the way you taught me, Hoss."

Clyde started hyperventilating. Twenty years. Twenty years without a ding. Without doing any time on the inside. If this night had never happened, Sid would have given Clyde a gold watch, and a nice funeral, and would have taken care of his wife and his mistress after the cancer had finished him off. Now he was on his way to being bait.

A fly landed on the end of his nose. It crawled on his face and lingered near the corner of his mouth. He saw Travis moving but it was as if he were watching through a keyhole. He felt someone kick him in the ribs and heard flies buzz around his head and the warm sticky hole in his gut. If only he'd had more time. He could have turned the kid. Could have taught him something. There'd been other cops before him. Lawyers. Judges. Politicians. There'd been plenty of others.

Travis thumbed something on his phone. "Is he dead?"

Travis's partner squatted down and looked Clyde in the face. "Almost."

"Good." Clyde heard Travis's voice, and the jingle of keys. "Get his feet."

✗

Tracy Falenwolfe's short fiction has appeared in *Spinetingler Magazine*, *Busted: Arresting Stories from the Beat*, and *A Bit of a Twist*, as well as online at *Crimson Streets* and *Flash Bang Mysteries*. She lives in Pennsylvania's Lehigh Valley. Learn more at www.tracyfalenwolfe.com.

RHONDA AND CLYDE

JOHN M. FLOYD

The strangest two days of Helen Wilson's life began with a ski-ing trip to Appaloosa Resort one winter Sunday. The trip itself wasn't unusual: Appaloosa was a popular location, and only forty miles from her home in the town of Lodgepole, Wyoming. What was unusual was that Helen had gone there in the company of friends. Helen Wilson didn't have many friends.

Even as a child she'd been a loner, and her school years had given her little reason to change. She also had no desire, after graduating with an accounting degree from UW, to leave her hometown to pursue a career. Instead she hired on as a bank teller, a safe and unpretentious job on a safe and unpretentious street near the house her late parents had left her. Ten years later Helen was still there, a sensible woman of reasonable means but no ambition, one of those rare people who doesn't require much in order to be happy. Even so, she was pleas-antly surprised when two total strangers engaged her in conversation one day at a neighborhood coffee shop, and even more surprised to find that she enjoyed their company.

Rhonda Felson and her husband Clyde were new to the area, Helen discovered—writers who had rented a cabin in the mountains nearby and who spent most of their time hiking and sightseeing and creating what Helen suspected would one day be masterpieces of lit-erature. During the days after that first meeting, the three of them had gotten together twice for dinner in local restaurants, and the following weekend Rhonda had invited Helen to accompany them to Appaloosa. The trip ended badly. Helen, who had never before been near a pair of skis, suffered the fate of many first-timers: six hours later she found herself medicated and hobbling on crutches through the exit doors of the local ER. More painful to her than her injuries was the knowledge that she'd been so much trouble to her new friends—they'd driven her to the hospital and then home afterward—and she found herself apologizing nonstop for spoiling their outing.

"Nonsense," Rhonda said, for the tenth time. She used Helen's key to open the apartment door and stood aside as Clyde helped her maneuver down the hallway to her bedroom. "These things happen. I'm just sorry it happened to *you*."

Helen sagged backward onto the bed, propped her bad leg up on pillows, and sighed. "Thanks, guys," she said. "I'll be okay now."

Rhonda was frowning. "Maybe I better stay. Clyde can come fetch me in the morning—"

"I'll be fine," Helen said again. "Oh, I just remembered—where'd we put my purse?"

"It's in the other room."

"Could you get it for me? My cell phone's inside it, and I need to call my boss."

"Now?" Clyde asked. "It's past ten."

"He stays up late. He knows a lot of the folks at the resort, and if he hears about my mishap, I want him to know I'll still be coming in to the bank tomorrow."

Both Felsons blinked at the same time. "You're going in to work?" Rhonda said.

"This isn't exactly life-threatening. I just want to forewarn him. I don't want everybody mooning over me when I limp in with my cast and my new wooden legs." Helen closed her eyes for a second and added, "Whoa—I can't believe I'm so tired."

"Tell you what. I'll make the call for you. You need to rest. What's your boss's number?"

Helen gave it to Rhonda and watched sleepily as the two of them left the room. It occurred to her that from now on she would stick to tennis….

* * * *

Sheriff Marcie Ingalls had never fully adjusted to cold weather. Her parents moved the family here from Alabama when she was nine, and she was sometimes convinced that she'd lived in balmy climes just long enough to thin her blood. But she'd married a local guy and her mother was still here, so Marcie made the best of it. She dressed in three or four layers, never complained, and even on subzero mornings usually got to the office before anyone else.

Today, though, she arrived to find the door unlocked and coffee brewing. Jerry Pearson, her only deputy, was at his desk in the back corner, feet propped up and a copy of *Guns & Ammo* in his hands.

"You're early," Marcie said. What a detective she would've made.

"And full of news," Pearson replied, in a bored voice. "I put a ticket on a car parked in the alley off Fourth Street, a twenty-foot limb fell from an oak in front of the courthouse, and the bakery has jelly donuts on special today."

Sheriff Ingalls shrugged out of her heavy coat and took a seat at her desk. "Was it blocking traffic?" she asked.

"What, the limb?"

"The car."

"No, just blocking the alley." Pearson tossed the magazine onto his desktop. "Illegally parked. You saying I shouldn't have ticketed it?"

"I'm just saying it's not even seven a.m., and nobody ever drives through there anyhow."

He snorted. "Where I come from, they'd tow it away."

"You're not where you came from, Jerry. We do things a little different, here."

"You can say that again." He nodded toward the window. "Hear that sound?"

Marcie frowned, listening. Sure enough, something was pounding on something, in the distance—BAM… BAM… BAM, sharp and clear in the brittle morning air. She was about to reply, then stopped as Wanda Stalworth, the dispatcher, pushed through the door in a bright red parka. They exchanged greetings, Wanda headed for her desk in the other room, and Marcie looked again at Jerry Pearson.

"I hear it," she said. "What is it? Hammering?"

"Yeah. Roscoe Three Bears. He's fixing Maude Jessup's front steps."

"Good. She's almost ninety, and that's a high porch—it'd be too bad if she fell."

"What I can't figure is why he does it. Splits her firewood for her, too. Roscoe's banned from the rez and dirt poor, and I hear she never pays him. Probably never even thanks him."

Marcie took a pair of reading glasses from her pocket and started riffling through her in-basket. "He does it because Maude's old and there's no one else to help her, Jerry."

He shook his head. "Maybe one of these days I'll understand that kind of thinking."

"I doubt it," she said.

From the dispatch desk Wanda called, "Are you two arguing again?"

"Not me," Pearson said. He rose to his feet and picked up his coat. "I'm going to do something to make me feel good, for a change."

"You quitting?" Marcie asked.

"Not that good."

"Where you going, then?"

"To buy some jelly donuts."

* * * *

Two hours later and two blocks away, in the bank on the corner of Western and Fourth, branch manager Spencer E. Spencer looked up from the papers on his desk to see loan officer Ernest Polk standing in his office doorway. Both men were wearing thick winter jackets, and Polk even had on a fur hat with earflaps. He looked like a movie poster for *Fargo*.

"Any word on the heating situation?" Spencer asked him.

"They're sending a repair crew from Casper," Polk said. "It'll take a couple hours. Until then I guess we'll just have to stay bundled up."

Spencer sighed. He had come in this morning to find the bank lobby as cold as Siberia, although the lights and the computers all seemed to be working. When he'd phoned the bank's home office, they had instructed him to call the heating-system people and to— above all else—remain open for business. He glanced through the glass wall of his office at two of his tellers, who were huddled at their stations like ice fishermen. Both were wearing mittens and had the hoods of their coats pulled up over their heads. He found himself dreaming of Florida.

Spencer E. Spencer was still staring at the lobby when his third teller clomped through the door on a pair of crutches. Helen Wilson was encased in a brown parka from the top of her head to her knees, and what little of her could be seen wasn't good: one eye was squeezed shut, her nose was bandaged, and a long comma of black hair hung in her face. Looking at no one and saying not a word, she solemnly made her way to her teller cage and wrestled herself onto her stool. The other two women muttered sympathetic words to her, their breath making little white clouds in the air, but otherwise the room was dead silent.

The two men in the office couldn't help staring. "She's in worse shape than I expected," Ernest Polk whispered.

Spencer, who had already alerted the staff, said, "That friend of hers—the one who called me last night to tell me Helen was coming in?—said she skied into a tree."

"She must've knocked it down."

"Tough lady," Spencer said. He reached for his phone and punched a number. When he saw Helen Wilson pick up her receiver, he said, "Sure you feel all right, Helen?"

"I'b vine," her voice said. "Doesn'd hurd doo bad."

"Looks like it would, from here. And what's wrong with your voice?"

"My doze is all stobbed up, dad's all. Like I god a gold."

"Okay," he said. "You let me know if you need anything." He hung up and said to Polk, "Maybe she'll have an easy morning—we shouldn't get many customers anyhow, with no heat."

But as soon as he uttered those words, the front door opened again and a short redheaded man entered carrying two duffel bags. On the nearest bag were the printed words PARADISE VALLEY CASINO. He walked to Helen Wilson's station, set the bags on the counter, and grinned at her. The tired smile she gave him in return looked more like a grimace, to Spencer, but the man didn't seem to mind. He also didn't seem bothered by the frigid temperature.

"Thank God for the casino," Spencer said. "They deposit more money in a week than most of our customers deposit in a year."

"I believe it," Polk said, as he turned to leave. "I'll keep a watch out for the repair folks."

Spencer nodded and went back to his paperwork, wishing he could do it with his gloves on. He also wished he didn't know the Paradise Valley Casino quite as well as he did. Sadly, some of those funds being deposited had probably once been his.

* * * *

It took him twenty minutes to sign off on the earnings reports and finish a long phone call with the bank's IT crew about an up-grade to his ATM software. Finally Spencer leaned back in his swivel chair, burrowed lower into his coat, looked over at the tellers—and frowned. No one was sitting at Helen Wilson's station. Earlier, around the time the casino courier was here, Spencer had noticed Helen leaving her stool to make several trips to the vault. That made sense: the casino's deposits were always large, and her crutches would prevent her from carrying too big a load at once. But now she was gone. He picked up the phone to call the head teller, but before he could hit the intercom button, Ernest Polk stuck his head into the office.

"Know what we should do, Spence?"

"What."

"We should have a promotion and give away those big duffel bags like the casino does."

"What?" Spencer said again. His mind was on injured employees, not bank giveaways.

"You know—those bags like the ones the guy was carrying earlier, with the name printed on the side. That's great advertising, and—"

"Wait a minute," he said, still holding the receiver. "Are you saying the casino lets anybody have those, for free?"

"Well, not free," Polk said. "You have to spend at least fifty bucks at the slot machines. But that doesn't take long."

Spencer frowned. A vague uneasiness had crept into his bones. Shaking it off, he said, "Thanks, Ernie. I'll consider it." Then, without waiting for a response, he pressed the button for the head teller and, when she answered, said, "Libby? Is Helen taking her break?"

"She left for home ten minutes ago, Spence. Said she wasn't feeling well after all. I'm not surprised—she shouldn't have tried to come in."

"Thanks, Lib. I'll give her a call." Which he did, after allowing her five more minutes to get home. That should be plenty—Helen's house was barely a mile from the bank.

But her cell phone didn't answer. It rang four times, then went to voicemail. Rather than leave a message, he found her home number and tried her landline. After three rings, she picked up.

"Helen?" he said. "It's Spencer, at the bank. Just wanted to make sure you're all right."

Helen Wilson said, a little groggily, "I'm fine—thanks for checking on me."

"Well, you sound better, anyway. More like yourself."

"Excuse me?"

"Your clogged nose," Spencer said. "It must've cleared up, right?"

Hesitation. Then: "It's my leg, Spence, not my nose. I broke my ankle."

"But—when you were here, earlier…."

"There? I wasn't there. I've been here at home all morning."

Spencer felt a cold ripple move through his stomach. "What?"

"My friend Rhonda phoned you last night, right? At first she was going to call and tell you I'd be coming in anyway, but she later said she'd taken the liberty of telling you I'd be staying home sick today. She was right, I guess—I needed the rest. So I stayed home."

Silence. Spencer tried to respond, but his throat seemed to have closed up.

"Didn't she call you?" Helen asked him. "What's going on?"

He swallowed. "I don't know. I mean—the person who called said you'd be coming in, like always. She didn't say anything about taking a sick day."

"Oh my. She must've misunderstood. Or maybe I misunderstood *her…*"

"Listen, Helen—this is important. Who's Rhonda?"

"I told you, a friend. I met her last week, she's the one who invited me to go skiing with her and her husband yesterday. The one who fell on my leg."

"Fell on it?"

"Well, it was an accident, but yeah, she fell and landed on my leg."

Spencer was sweating now, his heart thudding in his chest. "Hold on a second, okay?"

He rose and walked stiffly into the lobby and around to the teller area. Underneath the counter, in front of Helen's chair, he found it—a huge stack of bills. But they weren't bills at all—they were cash-sized bundles of blank paper. Helen's trips to the vault, he realized now, weren't to transport cash to it. They were to transport cash *from* it. If he'd been paying attention, he'd have noticed that the duffel bags the casino man had taken out of the bank were probably stuffed as full as they had been when he came in—but with real bills this time.

Quick as a flash, he pressed the alarm button under the counter, to alert the sheriff's department, then sprinted back to the phone in his office. "Helen?" he said. "What did they look like, your two friends?" But he was afraid he already knew.

"Look like? Well… the guy's short, reddish hair, glasses. His wife is—I don't know, about my height and weight, I guess. In fact it's a little spooky how much she does look like me, with the black hair and—"

"Names," Spencer blurted. "Do you have names?"

She gave them to him: Clyde and Rhonda Felson. He scribbled them onto a pad, looked up at the window, and saw Sheriff Ingalls's patrol car screech to a stop at the curb. As he leaped from his desk and hurried to meet the cops, Spencer realized he was trembling.

But not from the cold.

* * * *

"I can't believe it," Helen murmured. She was still propped up in her bed, her leg cast resting on a pillow. Her face was noticeably free of bruises and bandages. "Rhonda told me she told you I wasn't coming in… when in fact she told you I *was*. She was setting the stage for"—Helen swallowed hard—"for impersonating me."

Gathered around her were Sheriff Marcie Ingalls, Deputy Jerry Pearson, and branch manager Spence Spencer.

"That seems to be what happened," Marcie agreed.

Spencer, who seemed to have aged ten years, said, "You didn't hear her make the call?"

Helen shook her head. "No, she used my cell phone, from the other room. I was a little woozy anyhow, from the painkillers. But I remember her coming back in and waking me up and telling me you'd said that taking a day off was fine, and to get well soon."

"She must've been crazy, to stroll into the bank like that," Marcie said. "But it worked."

"Without that damn parka it wouldn't have worked," Spencer said. "Between it and the fake bandages, we couldn't see much of her face. Also, she disguised her voice."

"And her partner, husband, whatever—he walked out with… how much?"

Spencer shrugged. "We don't know yet. A lot." He ran a hand over his face. "With bags the casino gave him for free, for playing the slots. Insult to injury."

"You'll get me the security video, right?"

"Ernie Polk's holding it for you. And our main office has already offered a reward."

The sheriff nodded and looked at Helen. "Clyde Felson, you said? And Rhonda?"

"Yes." Helen repeated the descriptions she'd given to Spencer on the phone. "She really does look like me. She's prettier than I am, though." She sighed. "He called her Ronnie."

"Ronnie and Clyde?"

"Why not?" Deputy Pearson said.

Everyone turned to look at him.

Pearson shrugged. "They rob banks."

* * * *

Marcie and Pearson continued questioning Helen for another half hour, trying to come up with some kind of lead. The only thing helpful at all was the fact that the robbers and fake friends (Helen had to admit that's what they were) drove a black Toyota Tundra. At least that's the vehicle they'd taken Helen to the resort in. As for today, nobody remembered seeing what the imposter had driven to the bank.

Sheriff Ingalls said it had probably been Helen's Ford Focus, because of the possibility that someone *might* see it—and the fact that its keys were missing from her purse. In any case, the Ford was now parked in its rightful place behind Helen's house. The sheriff said they would check it over for prints, but that it would probably yield no clues; Rhonda Felson would almost certainly have kept her gloves on during the drive to and from the bank.

"Wait a second," Helen said. "I think they might've had *two* cars. One that I never saw."

"Why would you think that?" Marcie asked.

"We went to the resort in the Toyota, but Rhonda drove. Once, on Sunday, I saw Clyde take a set of keys from his pocket. It was only for a moment—he was looking for his ticket for the ski lift—but the biggest key on the chain wasn't for their Tundra."

"What kind of key was it?"

"A Honda."

"Are you sure?"

"Yes. It had that funny curved 'H,' that's bigger on top than on the bottom."

The sheriff and her deputy exchanged a look. Both were thinking the same thing: since the robbers knew Helen had seen the Toyota, they would probably ditch that vehicle someplace and use another for a getaway. They could always steal one, but if they already had a second car waiting in the wings…

"Okay, that helps. They're probably driving a Honda," Marcie said. "Anything else?"

"Not that I can think of." Helen heaved a sigh. "They even stole my crutches."

A silence passed. Marcie used it to look carefully around the room. When she noticed the old-fashioned telephone sitting on the floor between Helen's bed and the potty chair, she blinked.

"Helen, is that the phone you used earlier, to talk to the bank?"

"Yeah, Spence called me on it. I had to dig it out from under the bedside table. It's still connected, obviously, but I haven't used it much since I got my cell phone."

"Where's your cell phone now?"

"Same place as my crutches, probably. Rhonda used my cell to call Spence last night and must've kept it." Helen looked up and added, "I bet they figured they were taking my only phone, so I wouldn't be able to call anyone at the bank today—or get a call *from* anyone—and screw up their plans. They wouldn't have seen my landline."

The room fell silent again. Then Marcia had a thought.

"If your cell phone's still turned on," she said to Helen, "we can track it."

"It's still on," Spence E. Spencer said. "Or at least it *was*, after the robbery."

Everyone turned to face him. Marcie had actually forgotten he was still there, and then realized he was probably reluctant to go back to an unheated bank and a heated interrogation by his bosses. As he'd mentioned, he hadn't even determined yet how much money was taken.

"How do you know her cell phone's on?" she asked him.

"Because I tried to call her on it, first, and it rang. No one picked up, but it rang several times and went to voicemail—it didn't give me a 'not in service' message or anything."

"Okay," Marcie said, deep in thought. "That's good. We'll see if we can get the cell towers to triangulate the signal, try to pin down the whereabouts of the phone."

All of a sudden Helen's eyes widened. "You won't have to," she said.

"What?"

For the first time today, Helen Wilson smiled. "It has a GPS chip."

"Excuse me?" Marcie asked.

"A GPS locator. My aunt bought me the phone a few months ago and said if I ever lost it, this feature'll find it. There's an app that'll point us straight to it."

"How exactly does that work?" Pearson said.

"We just need Aunt Lettie's phone. It's tied to mine—you click the app on her phone, and it shows where my cell phone is, on a map. And where the Felsons are, if they still have it."

"Where does she live, your aunt?"

"Over past Battle Creek, near the edge of the reservation. About twenty miles—"

"I know her house," Marcie said. She pointed to the landline. "Will you call her?"

* * * *

Within minutes Sheriff Ingalls and her deputy were in her cruiser and headed for Lettie Wilson's home. As usual, Jerry Pearson sat silent and brooding in the passenger seat. Marcie glanced at him from the corner of her eye. She liked him but could never quite figure him out. He'd been a Seattle cop for years before moving here to be near his wife's folks and had always seemed either unable or unwilling to adapt to local ways. Marcie sighed. Here she was, in a high-stress/low-pay job, freezing her butt off every year between September and May, with a deputy who was always in a bad mood. She couldn't imagine two better examples of ducks out of water.

She forced her mind back to the matter at hand. "Something's worrying me here, Jerry," she said. "Remember what the banker said, about the heat being off, in the building?"

"I remember. What about it?"

"He said if it hadn't been off, if the imposter hadn't stayed bundled up in winter gear, he and the staff would've probably recognized that she wasn't Helen."

"And?"

"Seems pretty convenient," she said, "that heating-system failure."

Pearson lapsed again into silence. Then: "Are you thinking they—"

"I don't know." Marcie chewed her lip a moment. "But the people coming to fix it should be there by now. Why don't you call Wanda, have her connect you to the bank. Ask to speak to the head fred on the crew." She turned, and they locked eyes. "Humor me," she said.

Two minutes later they had the repairman on speakerphone.

"You fellas see anything strange?" Pearson asked him.

"Dern right we did," the guy said. "The wires were cut to the heating system."

Pearson blinked. "Did you say 'cut'?"

"Yep. As in 'severed.' Somebody took a crowbar to the panel door and cut the wires. The *correct* wires—nothing else was affected. Whoever did it knew his way around a power board."

"Where is this panel? Somewhere in the bank?"

"Above the bank. On the roof."

Pearson thanked the man, disconnected, and turned to the sheriff. "Whoa," he said.

"Sounds like they decided to improve their odds a bit."

"Sure does," Pearson said. "They get two bags with the casino's logo, find a bank employee with the right looks, befriend her, cause her to have a disabling accident, create a situation that makes a disguise even easier.... They know what they're doing, these two."

"So do we, now. We know one of them has teller experience and one's an electrician."

"Does that make us any closer to catching them?"

Marcie shrugged, her eyes on the road. "The more we know, the better off we are."

"We also know they're smart," he said.

"Let's hope they're not smart enough to turn off Helen's phone."

* * * *

Helen's aunt Lettie took a while to find her cell phone, but when she did, she loaned it to them with her blessing. Marcie and Pearson arrived back at Helen's apartment within an hour.

And found that they had company.

Two men in dark suits were standing in the bedroom. One of them, who looked like he'd just taken a bite out of a lemon, said, without a handshake, "Detective Murphy. State police." He pointed to his partner and added, "This is Detective Ellington. We'll take it from here."

Marcie glanced at Spencer, gave him a *Did you do this?* look. He shrugged and appeared clueless. She figured the big boys at the main bank had called the big boys in Cheyenne.

"I doubt you have the vast resources required for something like this," Murphy said.

Grinding her back teeth, Marcie said, "The crime happened in my county, Detective."

"But I suspect the criminals are no longer *in* your county, Sheriff." He looked down at the cell phone in Marcie's hand. "And it sounds like this will tell us for sure. Ms. Wilson, would you do the honors?"

Helen, still in bed, took her aunt's phone from Marcie, tapped some buttons, studied it a moment, and handed it back. Everyone crowded in to see.

On the screen was a map with a red dot in the middle. The location wasn't approximate; it was exact. According to the GPS, Helen's missing cell phone was now at an address on the northeast corner of Hill Street and Lancaster, in the small town of Florence. Sixty miles south.

They watched the screen for several minutes. The red dot didn't move.

Detective Ellington took out his own phone and Googled the address shown on the GPS map. After a moment he looked up at his partner. "Two-twenty Lancaster Street," he said, "is a place called the Traildrive Motel."

Murphy nodded, his eyes on the screen. The red dot stayed put.

"We got 'em," he said.

* * * *

Rhonda Felson, although that wasn't her real name, kicked off her shoes, stretched out on the too-small bed, and blew out a sigh. Her husband Clyde, although that wasn't his real name, hefted both duffel bags onto the rickety table in one corner of the room and stared at them lovingly. "So far so good," he said.

"I'm glad you're pleased," she murmured, her eyes closed. "I'll be pleased when we're in Florence, Italy, and not Florence, Wyoming."

"All in good time, Ronnie my dear."

Outside, the traffic on Lancaster Street, which consisted mostly of pickup trucks, was sparse. That was to be expected, probably: it was eleven a.m. on a weekday. But Clyde had a feeling traffic here was always sparse.

"So this is part of your plan?" she said. "Check into a motel only an hour away from the scene of the crime, in broad daylight?"

"This is one of the final phases of my plan," he said. "We're almost done, here."

"We'll be done, all right, if they find us."

He smiled, still looking at the bags. "They won't find us."

* * * *

Sheriff Marcie Ingalls pushed through the door of her office, tossed her hat onto the desk, and sagged into her chair. Deputy Pearson followed.

Seconds later Wanda Stalworth stuck her head in, from dispatch. "What are you guys doing back?" she said. "Did you catch 'em?"

"We're here because we were told to be," Marcie said. "It's not our case anymore."

"Then why are you frowning?"

Marcie rubbed her eyes. "Because something's bothering me." She looked all around, studying her surroundings if seeing them for the first time. "Something small, something I think we talked about, right here in this office. I just can't put my finger on it."

"You think the state cops are wrong, about heading down to Florence?" Pearson asked.

"I'm just saying we're missing something. As for Florence, those two detectives are in no hurry. I heard Murphy say he'll be taking several state troopers along with them and making this a big deal. He wants all the glory, I promise you that."

Pearson snorted. "While we stay here and write parking tickets. Right?"

Marcie blinked, then scowled. Slowly, she turned and focused on her deputy.

"What's the matter?" he asked.

"That's it. That's what I was trying to remember. That car you said you ticketed this morning, in the alley."

"What about it?"

"That alley runs beside the bank, Jerry. Right beside it."

"So?"

"And I bet there's a ladder on the side of the building, to the roof." They stared at each other for a long moment.

"The car," she said. "Was it a Honda?"

* * * *

Seventy-eight minutes later, Clyde Felson was relaxing in the room's only chair, reading a travel brochure he'd found in the drawer of the nightstand, while Rhonda counted the money in the two bags. She'd been counting for half an hour now.

In spite of Rhonda's doubts, the motel was everything Clyde had wanted: small, cheap, quiet, and perfectly located. He didn't plan to be here long.

He turned to Rhonda, idly watching the glow of the lamplight on her jet-black hair. He had just opened his mouth to speak to her when he heard the screech of tires somewhere outside the open window. A lot of tires. Then the slamming of car doors.

Clyde was on his feet in an instant, dashing to the window and easing the curtains aside to peek out.

The Law had arrived.

* * * *

Detective Michael Murphy was pleased with what he saw. As soon as he had assembled his team of patrolmen, they had hit the road and headed south. Now they were spread out evenly along the inside of the U-shaped row of twenty-four motel rooms. Ellington had already fetched the Hispanic owner—a man named Roberto Gonzales—from the motel office and had learned from the register that only one couple was checked in, at the moment: a Mr. and Mrs. Curtis Allen, from Laramie, in Room 12. Murphy was now standing outside that door, his weapon drawn and his mouth dry. As planned, he caught Ellington's eye and nodded once.

Ellington took Aunt Lettie Wilson's cell phone from his pocket and punched in Helen's number... and everyone went dead quiet. Helen had told them her ringtone was loud and distinctive: the "Throne Room" theme from *Star Wars*. Every cop on the scene held his breath, waiting and listening. Five seconds passed.

And then Murphy heard it. It was ringing. The phone was here.

But not behind the door of Room 12. The ringtone was coming from somewhere off to Murphy's left. He turned, alert and searching, and saw others turn as well. Moments later they found the source of the music: a small blue mailbox on the outside wall of the motel office.

Frantically Murphy signaled one of the troopers, who fetched a tire iron from the trunk of a cruiser and pried open the lid of the maildrop. Inside were half a dozen stamped envelopes and a model 5 iPhone, which had finally stopped playing John Williams's music and was now calmly instructing the caller, in Helen Wilson's recorded voice, to please leave a message.

But that wasn't all. Rubberbanded around the phone was a scrap of paper with the printed words:

PLEASE RETURN THIS TO HELEN. THANKS, AND ADIOS.

Murphy stared at it silently for a minute or more, ignoring the looks of his fellow cops and a confused-looking elderly couple standing in the now-open doorway of Room 12.

Detective Ellington and Mr. Gonzales were both peering over

Murphy's shoulder to study the message. Ellington looked at Murphy and asked, "Adios?"

"Si," Gonzales said.

* * * *

A hundred yards away, on the other side of Lancaster Street, the Felsons stood at the back window of Room 7 at the tiny Hamilton Inn, watching the festivities across the road. The room's curtains had been pulled back and the lights switched off so no one could see in from outside. Rhonda had brought Clyde the binoculars he'd placed on the bedside table an hour ago, and he was smiling as he watched the policemen in the Traildrive Motel's parking lot mill around, disperse, and leave the scene. When all activity had died down, he closed the curtains, switched the lights back on, and returned the field glasses to Rhonda's travel bag.

She stood there staring at him. "That was stupid. You know that, don't you? Stupid and risky. We should be miles away from here by now."

His gave her a smug look. "It was necessary. I wanted to know how safe we are."

"What do you mean?"

"I mean they sent the big guns after us. State troopers, suits, everybody at once. That tells me that pinpointing her phone with that app you saw on her screen—that was all they had. They know nothing else about us."

Rhonda didn't respond, but she did seem to relax a little.

"They'll never catch us now," he added. "We're home free."

"It was still stupid," Rhonda murmured.

He sat on the bed, put his shoes on, and laced them up. "Come on, let's get out of here."

"Thank God. I was afraid you'd want to stay the night."

"I've seen what I needed to see." He looked up at her. "We'll double back and be in Canada by tomorrow. Then, the world."

"Why'd you write 'adios,' on the note?"

"Misdirection never hurts," he said. "Whether they're after us or not."

Within two minutes they'd gathered their belongings. Rhonda handed Clyde her travel bag, then turned to leave the room key on the dresser. He looped the straps of the two casino bags over his shoulders, took his car keys from his pocket, and pulled open the door.

The gray Honda Accord was parked nose-out in the space directly in front of the room. Clyde pushed the button to pop the trunk even as he stepped out onto the sidewalk, his wife right behind him in the doorway. Head down and intent on his task, he loaded the two bags into the trunk, tucked Rhonda's bag in beside them, and closed the trunk lid.

And saw, for the first time, that he wasn't alone.

Two uniformed policemen, a man and a woman, were standing against the motel wall, ten feet from the door. The lady cop had a sheriff's badge, and her gun was drawn and pointed.

"Guess I don't have to ask if this is your car," she said.

* * * *

For a long moment the two suspects stood there, staring. Their expressions weren't scared, or angry, or even disappointed. Mostly, they looked stunned.

Marcie Ingalls said, in a level voice, "Turn around, both of you. Slowly. Hands behind your backs." She kept her automatic aimed and ready while Pearson cuffed them.

When they turned again to face her, the man—Clyde Felson, Marcie assumed—said, "How'd you know?"

She shook her head. "We didn't, at first. My deputy and I arrived at the other motel long before the cavalry did, and when we found that you weren't there, we looked around to see where else you might be. In case you decided to hide and watch from a distance."

"Watch? What made you think we might do that?"

"Nothing. But it happens sometimes, and it was worth a try." Without turning, she asked Deputy Pearson—who had already taken the car keys from Clyde—to check the bags. He opened the trunk and unzipped the two duffels.

"The money's here," he said.

"Main thing is," Marcie continued, "we knew you weren't at the other motel because your car wasn't in the lot. All we did then was check possible vantage points until we found it." She nodded toward the still-open doorway to Room 7. "The lady in the office confirmed that this was the room that went with the car."

"But—you had no way to know about our car."

Marcie smiled, took the parking ticket from her pocket, and held it up. "Yes, we did—not only the make and model, but the license plate number. Thanks to my deputy here, who wrote a citation for your Honda earlier today, in an alley beside the bank building. An alley with the only outside access to the roof." She smiled, watching their faces. "That was smart, disabling the heating system. Everything you did was smart, except for parking in the wrong place this morning and hanging around here too long now. Which, by the way, was downright foolish."

"I told you," the woman growled.

Clyde's jaw tightened. "Shut up, Ronnie."

Marcie took out her cell and called dispatch while Pearson finished checking the cab of the getaway vehicle. "Wanda? It's me," she said, into the phone. "Do me a favor. Track down Detective Murphy and tell him he might want to turn himself and his vast resources around and head back here to Florence. We have the two suspects in custody, along with the stolen cash. Yep, that's right. Tell him we're across the street from the red dot. He'll know what I mean."

She disconnected and turned to Pearson. "Find anything interesting?"

"A couple things." To the Felsons he said, "What kind of people steal a woman's crutches?"

Rhonda snorted. "Good old Helen. Guess she was at the wrong place at the wrong time."

"I agree," Pearson said. "And she was wrong about something else, too."

"What's that?"

"She told us you were prettier than she is."

Rhonda glared at him.

"Okay," Marcie said. "Let's go." Pearson gripped Clyde's elbow and steered him and his wife toward the cruiser.

"Ronnie and Clyde," Marcie added, walking behind them. "What are your real names?"

The man turned and gave her an even darker look. "Thelma and Louise."

Marcie smiled.

"They didn't end well, either," she said.

* * * *

Two days later things were back to normal. Around nine a.m. Sheriff Ingalls was sitting at her desk, sending an email to the mayor regarding his highly publicized but understaffed Pot-hole Prevention Program. For some reason, complaints about the poor condition of town streets were finding their way to the county sheriff instead of the city Public Works Department, and Marcie considered it her duty to place that particular monkey on the correct back.

Aside from the usual administrative headaches, though, all was going well. The quick arrest of the bank-heist suspects and the recovery of the stolen loot had put smiles on the faces of everyone except the two robbers and egg on the face of one Detective Michael Murphy. An additional but unexpected result of the incident was that the injured but wiser Helen Wilson now had an upcoming dinner date with Detective Scott Ellington. Proof positive, in Marcie's view, that clouds do have silver linings.

She had sent the mayor's email and was scrolling through the others when Wanda Stalworth ambled in from the other room. Marcie looked up, then turned back to her computer and said, "For what reason has the Wanda Woman abandoned her post?"

"Business is slow. Where's Pearson?"

"Out front, trying to fix our flagpole," Marcie said, eyes on her screen. A windstorm last night had snapped it off, along with three trees and the steeple of a nearby church.

Wanda, never one to be distracted from the important things in life, said, "Is that a box of donuts, on his desk?"

"Half chocolate, half cream-filled. Help yourself."

"You want one too?"

Marcie shook her head. "One of my rules: I only eat sugar when I hear good news."

"Why's that?"

"You got any good news?"

"I guess not."

Marcie nodded. "Well, there you go. It helps me stay skinny."

Wanda picked out a donut and took a bite. Chewing, she said, "I do have some gossip. I heard you told the bank folks that Jerry Pearson caught the robbers the other day."

"That's not gossip. It's a fact."

Wanda stared at her. "But he didn't, Sheriff. *You* solved the case— I was standing right here when you linked the criminals to the car that was parked beside the bank that morning."

"I didn't say Pearson *solved* it," Marcie corrected. "I said his actions led directly to their capture. If he hadn't ticketed that parked Honda, there would've been no record of the license plate, and we couldn't have found them." She leaned back in her chair, holding

Wanda's gaze. "If law officers were eligible for such things, I'd have made sure Pearson got that reward the bank offered. And I'll tell you something else: If it'd been me, I wouldn't even have written that ticket. Pearson did what he felt was right, and it turned out to be the only thing that pointed us to the guilty party."

Wanda finished her donut and wiped her mouth with a napkin. When her hand came away, Marcie saw that she was smiling.

"What's so funny?"

"I seem to remember you hinting, that morning, that Pearson should change his way of thinking."

"Well, I take it back," Marcie said. "I'm not sure I *want* him to change."

Wanda seemed to consider that, then said, "You might be a little late."

"Why?"

"Because of the reward." Wanda tossed the wadded-up napkin into a trashcan and sat down on the edge of Pearson's desk. "Do you recall telling us, yesterday, that the bank had withdrawn the reward offer because no one had come forward with information leading to the arrest and capture, blah blah blah?"

"Yes," Marcie said. "What about it?"

"Libby Anders, the head teller at the bank, called me this morning. She said Deputy Pearson told the bank manager last night that the reward would have to be paid. Said that he—Jerry Pearson—was informed by two alert citizens early Monday morning that a strange car was parked in the alley beside the bank. Said he wouldn't have noticed it otherwise. Since information from that ticket, as you said, later led to the apprehension of the two suspects, Pearson insisted that those two people should be given the full reward. Ten grand, divided between them."

"Who were these two observant citizens?"

"Roscoe Three Bears and Maude Jessup."

Marcie blinked. "You're kidding."

"Nope. Pearson said they mentioned the illegally parked car to him on his way to the office that day. Then he walked over and wrote the ticket."

"But...." Marcie stared into the distance, thinking. "Roscoe was working on Maude's house at the time. Repairing her porch steps. To even talk to them, on his route to work, Pearson would've had to climb three fences and cross two yards."

Wanda narrowed her eyes. "Are you wondering if that's what really happened?"

"Well... I'm wondering what Roscoe and Maude would say, if asked about it."

"Pearson said they shouldn't have to be contacted."

"What?"

"He said Roscoe doesn't speak much English, and Ms. Jessup forgets things sometimes."

Marcie thought that over, and felt a smile spread across her face. Slowly she rose from her chair and crossed the room to the front window. On the snow-covered lawn between the office and the street, a man in a furry brown coat stood surrounded by tools, his fists on his hips and his eyes on a new brace that had been bolted to the pole supporting the Stars and Stripes.

Marcie stared out the window at her deputy for a long moment. *Flagpoles aren't the only things you can fix, are they, Jerry?* She was surprised at the sudden warmth she felt in her heart.

"That sounds reasonable to me," she murmured.

"What?" Wanda said.

Before Marcie could reply, she caught a glimpse of Helen Wilson's maroon Ford. She saw it putter its way up the snow-cleared street and pull into a parking spot, saw Helen climb out and limp on her recovered crutches to the front door of the bank. Spence Spencer appeared then, as if he'd been waiting for her to arrive. Marcie watched as he held the door open for Helen, bowed theatrically, and followed her inside. First, though, Spencer turned and stared directly down the street, at the sheriff's office. Directly at *her*. Marcie knew he probably couldn't see her from that distance, but he raised a hand anyway, and so did she. She thought she saw a grin on his face.

"What was it you just said?" Wanda asked again.

Marcie blinked and turned from the window. "I said I think I'll have a donut after all."

"Chocolate or cream-filled?"

Once more, Marcie felt herself smile. "One of each."

✗

John M. Floyd's short stories have recently appeared in *Ellery Queen Mystery Magazine*, *The Strand Magazine*, *The Saturday Evening Post*, and *The Best American Mystery Stories 2018*. He is an Edgar nominee, a three-time Derringer Award winner, and the author of seven collections of short mystery fiction.

THE IDEA
CHARLIE HUGHES

Jessica Peterson-Brown shifted into third and put her foot down, propelling her SUV past the car in front. She maintained pressure on the pedal, arrowing down the country road.

This needed to be over as soon as possible. Get there, find out what the hell he wanted and get out.

Was it wrong to think in those terms, about a man who'd suffered such a terrible misfortune? Gerald Stevens was a shit of the highest order, and it would take more than a car crash for her to revise that opinion.

His home loomed into view as the car ascended a hill. A tall, substantial townhouse, incongruously set in the Warwickshire countryside. She'd seen it twice before. Once to attend a party organized by his agent, the second, to confront him over an affair with a much younger author, a friend of Jessica's of whom she was particularly protective. On this latter occasion, she'd changed her mind at the last moment and continued to Stratford Upon Avon. The affair ended, but not before Stevens reduced the woman to a shell of her former self.

Perversely, they were considered respectful rivals. Peerless contemporaries, pursuing a creative duel which drove them both to new heights.

She recalled Hodder purchasing her debut novel *Devil Season* all those years ago. They sent advance copies to particular authors to generate buzz. In response, Stevens wrote her a letter, a handwritten note in which he identified numerous plot holes and weaknesses in her writing style. To receive such a thing from an established author had been a bitter blow. She took weeks to see it for what it was: a spiteful grenade tossed in her direction, intended to shatter her confidence.

Devil Season became a bestseller, which turned into a hit film, prompting a lucrative book deal. The letter was forgotten, but Gerald

Stevens would not recede so quietly from her life.

Over the years, a pattern emerged. She did her best to avoid crossing paths with him, while he did the opposite. Stevens turned up to the same parties, wrote reviews of her novels in the press, even dated her friends. Most irritatingly of all, two years ago, he switched agents and took up with the same firm as her.

She turned the SUV through the gates and into the long gravel driveway. In the distance, she spotted Stevens' daughter waiting at the expansive front door.

Jessica recalled their peculiar phone conversation.

"He wants to see you. He's weak. We don't know how long it will be," Alison Stevens had said.

"I wouldn't want to disturb him. Not at this time."

"He says it's important, crucial somehow." The desperation in the young woman's voice hit home. Imagine growing up with Gerald Stevens for a father.

By the time Jess had parked and stepped out of the car, Alison was approaching.

"Thank you. Thank you so much," she said.

There were bags under her eyes, her hair was a mess, but beneath the burdens of her father's accident, Jessica noted her delicate good looks.

"How is he?" she asked, embracing Alison.

The young woman stood back and shook her head. "He has the best care money can buy. But he's here, at home, for a reason. The doctors say it's only a matter of time."

They walked into the house and up four flights of stairs. "He wants to see the hills," Alison explained, "so we put his bed in the study."

At the top of the stairway, they walked down a long corridor and reached a large door. Alison and drew herself up with a long inward breath. She opened the door and stood to the side. "He wants to see you alone, undisturbed. You can tell the nurse to come out."

Jessica entered the room. Ahead, she could see a large set of glass doors opening onto a balcony. Thick, dark clouds obscured the landscape beyond.

As she went further into the room, it opened out to reveal a four-poster bed surrounded with tethered pumps and drips.

To the side, a young female nurse sat on a chair, immersed in the screen of her mobile phone.

She looked up, frowned and put her finger to her lips. "Not now.

He's sleeping."

Jessica was about to retreat when a weak but irritated voice rose from the bed.

"Who put you in charge, silly bitch?"

On closer inspection, Jessica detected the bandaged head buried among the pillows and bed linen.

The nurse said, "Mr. Stevens. I'm responsible for ensuring you…"

"You're responsible for nothing. Now leave us alone to talk."

Jessica could see the woman wrestling with her pride, then relenting. Walking past, she said, "You've got ten minutes."

When she was gone, Jessica moved closer, standing over the bed. Her disdain for the man wavered. There was nothing left. He was pale, almost blue. Tubes extended from his nose and mouth. On his arms, resting above the sheets, loose skin melted over the bones.

"I haven't eaten in four weeks," he said, as if reading her thoughts. "I was crushed. Did you know?"

"I did," she said. "I'm so sorry, Gerald."

"Stomach won't hold anything but liquid. It's a mess under here."

Looking down at the twisted shape beneath the sheets, she shivered. "I'm so, so sorry."

"I'm going to die. They aren't sure when, but soon."

Not knowing what to say, she dropped her eyes. When the silence became intolerable, she said, "Gerald, why did you ask me…?"

"Sit down, woman. Sit down."

She did as instructed. It was odd how such a little thing, an impoliteness, a reminder of his brusque manner, could bring back the enmity.

"I asked you here because we're friends." he said.

She mulled this for a moment, "No. I don't believe we are, Gerald."

He spluttered, and for a moment she thought he was having a seizure. She realized he was laughing.

"That's what I like about you," he said, "honesty. It shines through in your writing."

She said nothing in response, eager to avoid diversions.

When the wheezing subsided, he continued. "I've always sensed you look down on my work, Jessica. A lack of respect for my end product. Is that fair?"

"We're very different writers."

"That's not what I asked."

She sighed, "Gerald, I am so sorry. For the pain you are in and the pain this must cause your family. But I do not understand why I'm here. Why I have been…" she paused, then said it, "…summoned?"

"I'm taking up your time? You must be busy with your next novel."

He always knew where to sting.

She thought of the email she'd received from her agent that morning. A breezy greeting, an unamusing anecdote about a visit to the gym, followed by the inevitable enquiry: "How's the novel coming along? Anything you can send me?"

"I'm just curious," Jessica said. "I'd like to assist, if I can."

"You can help me, and you can help yourself." A broad smile stretched across his face.

Jessica shifted in her chair. "How?"

"You're one of the few people who'll understand. I'll do my best to give this some… context."

Whatever his injuries, Stevens could still move. He shifted up in the bed so his head could turn towards her.

"You know those moments," he said, "when an idea comes, when the nuts and bolts of a story form in the mind's eye?"

She nodded.

Stevens went on, "One minute you're thinking about the weather and the next, it hits you. Wham! And if it's a good one, a really good one, it's exhilarating, right?"

"Sure. That's happened," she said.

"Until recently, I never had to work at it. They just came. Some better than others, sure, but they arrived nice and regular."

This was the first time he'd spoken to her about their craft. It brought him to life, a flickering light behind the eyes.

"That's the part of the job I love the most. When the ideas come, nothing else seems important. I have to do them justice."

"You did, Gerald. You can be proud."

"But they dried up."

For a terrifying moment, Jessica thought he might burst into tears.

"Did that happen to you?" he went on. "Did they stop coming?"

"No," she lied.

"Something about me. Something about my lifestyle meant the production line ground to a halt," he said.

"It can happen."

"I went two years with nothing useable. I rehashed old set-ups.

I went back over my notes from my younger days and found a few things. But I couldn't do it anymore."

"That's tough, Gerald, but where do I come in?"

"Wait, wait. Let me tell you the whole thing. Grant me that."

She raised an apologetic hand.

He continued, "Four weeks ago I was driving home from London. I'd had meetings with my agent and publisher. I was in a good mood. HBO were enquiring about my Linton James series, more meetings to come, but it looked promising."

He turned further onto his side, grimacing. When he settled, he looked up at her and smiled again. She couldn't say what troubled her about this, but she was more certain than ever that Gerald Stevens was not a man to trust.

"I was passing a set of fields. Just pasture. Big green squares with nothing distinctive about them. Something made me turn and look. A tiny movement in the corner of the field. It was a man wearing head-phones, wielding a metal detector. In that split second, something clicked. It was the trees, it was the field, it was something my agent had said the day before, but most of all, it was the image of that lone man, searching for something in the field.

"It all came together, and I mean everything. As if it had built up over the last few years, water against a dam. When it broke, it was majestic. In the space of a second, I had it all. The main character, the terrible people he would ally with, the human motivation at the heart of the story. This wasn't just good. This was the best I'd ever had."

He was breathless, panting with excitement.

"So I had to get home, it was desperately important for me to get home and write as soon as possible. And you know what happened next?"

She tilted her head. "The accident, on the bridge."

"Two miles from home. It was all my fault. I was driving too fast, not concentrating."

"And me? What does this have to do with me?"

"I'm in too much pain. These tubes keep me alive, it can't go on. But I need to know the idea is safe. I want this novel written, and I have to leave it in capable hands."

"You want me to write it? Gerald, thank you, but I do my own stuff."

"You've never done anything this good. Trust me. Word on the street is, you've dried up."

She drew breath and closed her eyes.

He continued, "I'll tell you the story, and the novel comes out under joint authorship."

"Gerald, I'm going now." She stood and turned to walk away.

His voice broke to a higher note. "Just…. Let me tell you the idea. Just hear me out."

Jess stopped and looked up at the ceiling, knowing she would regret walking out on a dying man. She returned to her chair. "Tell me."

"Thank you." He took a long, deep breath, "That nurse is a nosy cow, I don't even want Alison to hear this." The glimmer of light returned to his eyes. "Come closer."

She leaned in, over the bed.

He began in a whisper. "It goes like this…"

* * * *

Jessica's eyelids were heavy, but she couldn't switch off.

During the train journey to Manchester, she'd argued on the phone with her partner, Seamus. He'd been badgering her for weeks about a holiday. She needed to get her novel moving, she told him, and couldn't even think of going away.

"I'll go on my own," he'd said and hung up.

At the literary convention, they interviewed her on stage, playing the role of the successful, affable novelist. She left the post-event drinks early, claiming to have a headache, and returned to her hotel in Piccadilly.

She used the time to fill six pages on her notepad, developing her latest idea. Even as she worked, she could feel her enthusiasm ebbing. The story would fail, just like all the others.

The digital clock read 3:23 a.m. in fierce red numerals.

Each time the conversation with Gerald Stevens hopped into her mind, Jess tried to push it aside.

He'd been right, and it infuriated her. In the space of five sentences that unpleasant man had unveiled the foundations of an original, electrifying story. The central character and plot twist opened so many possibilities. Done right, the way she would do it, the book would be a heavy, dark tome, almost sliding into horror. It would sell and sell big.

From her bed, Jess could see the tiny green standby light of her laptop poking out of its bag.

She climbed out from beneath the sheets and snatched it up.

Opening the laptop on the desk, it revealed the notes she'd written earlier. Jessica closed the file and opened a new document.

She wrote:

"The Cleansing Soil."

It was a good title, but it belonged to someone else.

She typed again:

"By Jessica Peterson-Brown."

Jess tapped at the keyboard and didn't stop until the cleaner came to the door five hours later.

* * * *

Jessica breezed into the London offices of Jenkins and Wilmore Associates.

The receptionist told her which executive meeting room to use, then gave her a guilty smile.

"Look, I know I'm not supposed to do this," the receptionist said, "but could you sign my copy of Together, Forever?"

Jessica gave her a beaming smile. "Let's have it."

She could be uncomfortable in these situations, but not today. When the receptionist gushed with praise, Jess told her how pleased she was that her agent employed such loyal fans.

In the meeting room, she helped herself to coffee and a pastry.

Dina Wilmore poked her head around the door, lips pursed in mock surprise. "My good God!" she said and swept into the room.

Dina was a large, attractive woman, accustomed to dominating her surroundings. Jess thought of her as a protectress, a wily mother bear who'd do anything to shield her cubs.

They embraced, and Dina said, "It's brilliant, Jess." They sat down on the same side of the table. "It's not brilliant, it's astounding."

"Thank you. That means a great deal."

"How on earth did you think of it? The ruse, it's breathtaking."

Jess looked into her paper cup. "Sometimes, they just come."

"Well, if the first six chapters are anything to go by... I don't want to predict what could come of this. You'll have something special."

Dina stood and got them both fresh coffee.

Jess said, "We should send it to Hodder, so they know what's coming."

"Well, that's an option."

Jess narrowed her eyes. "Oh."

"Don't waste this on them, Jess."

"This is the only thing I have, and I owe them one more. There isn't a spare in the trunk," Jess said.

"True. But we need to think about this. We could, you know, not deliver."

"Just like that?"

"How can I put this? They've been worried for a while," Dina said. "We all have. For six months, I've been telling them a draft is on the way."

Jess shrugged. "It can take time."

Dina waved her hand. "If we approach them with a deal, if we say the next book isn't coming, we can get out of it. It will take some wrangling, but I can do it." She smiled. "I might have held initial, informal conversations."

"Dina!"

"You blame me? Only a month ago I was getting radio silence. I thought the wheels had come off. In a way, it's worked out well."

Jess shook her head. "Where are you going with this?"

"It's the perfect alibi. Hodder thinks you're struggling. All we're doing is confirming it. We do a deal, but we forget to mention we have the novel of the decade burning a hole in our pocket."

Jess liked it when Dina got this way. She could think of nobody else she'd rather have on her side.

"It's my job to look out for your interests." She approached, standing over Jess and moving her head up close, their noses almost touching. Dina spoke in a low, confident voice. "You finish *Cleansing Soil*, and we take it to an open market. We'll have them eating out of our hand."

"I'll think it over," Jess said.

"I knew you were great. I did. I've always loved your work. But this," Dina raised her palm above her head, "this is next level." Her agent giggled. "They will *remember* you for this."

* * * *

Gerald Stevens's death was greeted with howls of despair from his fans and relative indifference in the world of art and entertainment.

#RIPGerald was trending on Twitter for two days, but the BBC spent just thirty seconds on the subject for the evening news. Print obituaries, lengthy though they were, lacked the warmth often conjured for the passing of a favored son or daughter. By the time his fu-

neral came around, the churn of news and comment had moved along.

Jessica took the news in her stride. She put out a short but generous statement via Dina. By happy coincidence she was making a promotional visit to Sweden on the day of his funeral. She sent flowers and got on with writing her novel.

Returning to her South London home, Gerald Stevens couldn't have been further from her thoughts.

The next morning, Jessica was working at her desk when she glanced out of the second-floor window. She saw a woman walking down the street, turning to look at Jess's home. For a full-minute Jess failed to place her and when she did, she was more confused than concerned. The woman walked on, and Jess continued writing.

She left the house at 10 a.m. to pick up her dry cleaning. On her way back, she saw the woman again, this time walking straight towards her.

Gerald Stevens's nurse retained the same irritated expression and slouching demeanor Jess recalled from their first meeting.

When they met on the pavement, the nurse said, "Hello, Jessica."

"Hello. This is a coincidence."

The woman looked over Jess's shoulder. "Could we go somewhere?" She nodded towards the house.

Jess said, "We can go for a coffee, 'round the corner."

The woman rolled her eyes. "Fine."

They entered the coffee shop. The nurse sat at a table, leaving Jess to get the coffees. When she returned with them, her new companion still wore her overcoat; both hands jammed into the pockets.

Jess said, "So, Nurse...?"

"Nurse will do."

"Nurse Nurse it is," Jess smirked.

Slowly and deliberately, the woman leaned forward and said, "You're very sure of yourself, aren't you?"

Jess had not expected such hostility. "Are you here to cause trouble?"

"I've got information." The nurse took her hands from her pockets and picked up her coffee. "Information you'd be very interested to hear. It's about the thing Mr. Stevens told you."

Jessica felt a pulse of heat rising around her ears. "Okay. So tell me."

"Not as easy as that, is it?"

"Why?" Jess asked.

"Because," the nurse widened her eyes, "we need to make an arrangement."

"An arrangement?"

The nurse raised her hand, rubbing her forefinger and thumb together.

Jess sat back. "Blackmail?"

The woman shook her head. "It isn't blackmail, I checked. I'm just offering to give you information, for a price."

Jess glanced down at her hands, wondering if the woman could see them shaking. "And how can I decide if I want to hear this?"

"You will."

"How much?"

"Twenty thousand."

Jess scoffed, "Oh. come on. Be serious."

"Trust me, lady. When I tell you, you'll wonder why I didn't ask for more."

"I need more."

"I'll give you a taster. Just a little one, mind."

Jess felt cold air on the back of her neck. The door of the shop had opened behind her.

The nurse's face dropped. "I've got to go." She pushed a card across the table. "I've got to go now."

Jess turned to see a man entering. She'd never seen him before. He was tall and broad shouldered, with a pock-marked complexion and razor short hair. He wore an expensive black suit. The man went to the counter, paying no attention to either Jess or the nurse.

When Jess turned back, the nurse was gone, scurrying down the street.

* * * *

Dina Wilmore stood in Jess's kitchen and spoke slowly to her client. "You're making no sense."

"The nurse. She wants money. Then this guy comes in, and she got spooked, and that was it."

"Okay, stop. Don't say another word." Dina's voice was firm, reassuring. "Sit down and say nothing. I'll make us both a cup of tea, and when I come back to this chair, I want you to start at the beginning. Then slowly, calmly, tell me everything that's happened. Can you do that, Jess?"

"Yes." Jess sat down. When the tea appeared, she did as instructed, leaving nothing out.

* * * *

Dina said, "So let me get this straight. You took an idea Gerald Stevens gave you, an idea for a novel he wanted joint credit for. You told him you didn't want to write it, but now you are. And his nurse wants money from you because she knows you took his idea."

Jessica closed her eyes, unable to look at her agent. Then she heard the laughter. She opened them, irritated at first, then relieved to see Dina's mirth.

"What? What?" Jess said.

"That's what you're so upset about?"

"There might be more. The nurse gave me this card. She told me to contact her."

Dina stopped laughing and returned to her motherly tone. "Jess, you've done nothing wrong. If Gerald Stevens wanted to write this novel, he shouldn't have driven his car into a river, should he?"

Dina went on. "Writers swap ideas all the time. They steal, they rewrite, they often plagiarize. Some of the things I could tell you! And most of the time they get away with it."

She was on a roll now, striding around the kitchen, flailing her arms. "All you've done is listen to a bitter dying man and built something beautiful on the foundations of his idea. If some nurse thinks that's worth blackmailing you for, I'll call the police myself. Give me that card. I'll put the wind up her."

Jess handed it over.

"But what if people find out it's not my idea?"

"Darling, half of Shakespeare came from the Greeks." She laughed again. "Nobody cares."

"Sure?"

"You're so close to finishing this, Jess. You just need to close it down with a flourish. I can't tell you how exciting this is. Don't let this throw you off course. Please."

Jess stood, walked across the kitchen and hugged Dina. "Thank you."

* * * *

Jess emailed Dina the final chapters of *Cleansing Soil* twelve days later. It was an exquisite moment.

Everything in the novel bore her stamp. The compelling narrative arc, the rich textured characters, the shocking denouement were all unmistakably Peterson-Brown.

Except, *Cleansing Soil* was more than that. Her career had been a long, arduous journey towards this point. This was the novel she had always wanted to write, but never quite achieved.

They *would* remember her for this.

Her agent had been her first reader for many years. It was normal for Dina to wait a few days before giving her verdict. In Dina's words, it helped to "let it percolate."

On the fifth day, Jess couldn't wait any longer. She needed her optimism confirmed. She called Dina's mobile and got no answer.

Jess tried Dina's office number and a woman picked up. "Jenkins and Wilmore. How can I help?"

"I was trying to get hold of Dina. It's Jess Peterson-Brown."

There was silence at the other end of the line. A muffled rustling, the line went silent, then a man's voice came on.

"Hello, Jess." It was Dina's business partner, Howard Jenkins.

"Always a pleasure, Howard, but I wasn't expecting to speak to you."

In a shaky voice, he said, "Jess, there's something odd going on."

"Odd?" she said.

"With Dina. She's gone AWOL. Nobody can get hold of her."

"She unwell?" Jess asked.

"Worse. We've received letters." He coughed. "Letters from her lawyers and accountants."

"I don't get it."

"She's divesting herself. Pulling out of the partnership and taking her money and shares with her."

Jess tightened her grip on the handset.

Jenkins continued, "It's embarrassing for me to ask, but I know you were close."

"We were. We are."

"Did Dina say anything? Did she mention she was even thinking of doing this?"

Jess shook her head.

"Hello? Jessica?"

"No. Nothing."

Jenkins said, "I know she was under a lot of stress, but I had no idea this was on the cards."

Every time Jenkins spoke, it jarred with Jess. "She seemed relaxed to me. Same old bubbly Dina," she said.

Howard said nothing, his breathing still audible. Jessica spoke, "Howard, why did you think she's been stressed?"

"Well, she's had some financial problems. She always struggled to keep her spending under control, but it had been getting worse. And then there was your..." He stopped. "Your work, Jess. The dip in productivity."

Jess laughed, but even she could hear the nervous edge. "My productivity? I've finished. Dina's reviewing the draft."

He said, "She's been telling me for months that you couldn't get anything to work."

"No, no. I've been writing a novel called *Cleansing Soil* for the past six months. She didn't mention it?"

He gave a pained sigh. "This gets stranger. I spoke to Dina on Friday. She said some harsh things, Jess."

"About what?"

"About you."

"No," Jess said. "You've got this wrong."

"You're 'dried up.' That's what she said. 'All dried up.'"

Jess thought of Gerald Stevens using the same words.

Jenkins said, "Jess, could you send me the draft? I think that'll help clear a few things up."

He was a smooth operator, but Jess knew what he meant. He didn't know who to trust, and the draft would tell him which way to jump.

She spoke calmly, the way Dina liked. "Okay, Howard. Give me ten minutes, and I'll email it over." She hung up.

Jess went upstairs and turned on the PC. She waited for the log-in screen, but instead of launching in the usual way, white text on a black background appeared.

System Error. Load operating platform.

Jess whispered to herself, "No." Panic was inching towards the surface.

It's fine, she thought, the back-up is safe on the cloud. This thing with Dina is all a misunderstanding. And the emails sent to Dina would be in her Gmail account. Thank God for remote access.

She pulled her iPad off the shelf and opened it up. Jess tapped on the iCloud icon. When it requested her log-in details, she typed her usual username and password.

Error. Account does not exist.

She typed it in again, more carefully this time.

Error. Account does not exist.

Her breathing became heavier and faster. She put her hands over her mouth and tried to breathe her own air. After a minute, she tapped on the iPad again and switched to the Gmail App. Again, it asked her to log-in. As she typed in her credentials, a creeping feeling of dread grew in her stomach.

Account not recognized.

She typed again, and again.

Account not recognized.

On the twelfth attempt, a low, painful groan escaped her.

Jess tried one more time. When the error message came back, she picked up the tablet and threw it against the wall.

* * * *

Jess followed the woman by foot, dodging the Baron's Court traffic and trailing her down the road. Fresh wisps of breath danced in front of her, yellowed by the streetlights.

She'd discovered Lucy Alford's workplace by phoning nursing agencies and impersonating Alison Stevens. She couldn't recall the name of the nurse who'd provided such wonderful care for her father, she said, but wanted to write a thank you note. The fifth agency she called took the bait. They would not give a home address but shared the location of a private hospital in West London.

The woman turned into West Kensington Tube. Jess followed through the barriers. So late at night, there were few people around. On the platform, she tailed Alford onto a train and sat down opposite her.

It took two stops on the District Line before Alford looked up from her phone.

"Well, well, well," Alford said and leant forward. "Now you want to talk?"

"What were you going to tell me? I need to know."

"That ship has sailed, m'love."

Jessica sprang forward. She grabbed the lapels of Alford's jacket and pushed her back into the seat. "Tell me."

Alford said nothing and the train pulled into a platform. When the doors opened, an elderly man in green overalls stepped onto the carriage. Jess pulled away and sat down next to Alford.

"I'm sorry," she said. "I'm under a lot of pressure."

"I gave you a chance. You could have called, but they got in first."

"Who is they?"

Alford said, "You don't know a thing. The daughter, the agent."

None of this should have surprised Jessica, but to hear it first hand was shocking. She was lost in this thought when Alford spoke again.

"I asked them for twenty. They gave me twenty. It's what you should have done."

"They gave you twenty thousand pounds?"

"When they realized I knew what they had planned, yeah. To keep my mouth shut. That's what I intend to do."

Jess stared at the woman, but she was thinking of her novel.

At the next stop, Lucy Alford stood and spoke over her shoulder. "They used you, idiot. To write the book." She smiled. "Contact me again, and I'm calling the police."

* * * *

Jess sat on the easy-chair in her dressing gown, watching a program about second homes on the Mediterranean. She didn't understand why it was on her television.

Her doctor had prescribed Diazepam to be taken twice daily. Seamus told her this was a positive step, "The first stage in recognizing a problem." He'd moved out a few weeks before but rang every day. He still loved her, he said, but refused to return until she was over "this Gerald Stevens thing."

She got muddled over the pills. She might have taken her dosage today, but she wasn't sure.

The doorbell rang, but Jess didn't rise from the sofa. Only when Howard Jenkins' voice sounded through the letter box did she realize someone was there.

"Hey, Jess, it's Howard."

He'd arranged to come 'round, but wasn't it supposed to be tomorrow? Jess went to the door.

When she opened up, Jenkins wasn't alone. Alison Stevens stood next to him, her arms folded. Behind her was a man she recognized but could not place. He wore an expensive black suit with razor short hair. His pock-marked skin made her think of rotten cherries.

The combination of faces felt wrong to Jess, but she couldn't think what to say. She stood to one side, and they filed into her home.

In the living room, clothes, mugs and plates covered the sofa and chairs. They stood awkwardly searching for someplace to sit.

"Sorry," Jess said, "the mess."

Howard said, "It's okay." He gestured, and the others shifted the debris to sit.

Jess sat down in her own seat. "Why are you here?" she asked. There was no antagonism in her voice. She just wanted to know.

Jenkins touched Alison Stevens's shoulder. "Jess, I think you know Alison." Then gestured towards the man in the suit with the bad skin. "This is John Hargrove. He's been the lawyer to the Stevens family for many years." He fiddled with the pleat in his trousers. "We came because we've been having some discussion, about how this whole situation came about."

"My book, you mean?" Jess said. Even through the haze created by the pills, she held onto that. The book was hers, and someone had taken it from her.

"Well, the claims you've been making," Jenkins said. "We want to clear a few things up."

The lawyer cut in. "Gerald Stevens met with you, Ms. Peterson-Brown. Nobody denies that. He met with you before he died, to say goodbye to a friend. You seem to have taken on some, some fantasy about writing a novel. A piece of work that he is somehow linked to."

Jess nodded. "He had the idea. I wrote it."

Alison Stevens was shaking her head, "Have you ever lost someone close, Jessica? It's distressing enough. What you're doing is ghastly."

Jess shrugged, "What am I doing?"

Alison Stevens put her hands to her cheeks. "You followed me! For days."

"Did I?"

"Yes. You accosted me, violently, in a supermarket car park. Security had to pull you away."

Jess recalled something like this happening. As with everything else recently, it didn't feel like something that should have happened to her.

Jess said, "Someone took my novel. It was you and Dina."

The lawyer spoke again. "Ms. Stevens and her family would be well within their rights to go to the police."

"And the press," Alison said.

"Hey, hey!" Jenkins was bobbing up and down in his seat. "We don't want this to become a slanging match. We agreed to that."

Jessica bowed her head and sobbed.

Alison Stevens rolled her eyes. "Oh, Christ."

Howard put his arms around Jess. "Look, Jess, we can clear this up. You met with Gerald, and you talked. Maybe you spoke about a novel. And yes, he has one more coming out."

The lawyer leaned forward in his chair. "Given the raw feelings over this, and your hitherto good reputation, my clients do not wish this matter to progress this through the courts," He turned to look at Alison, "or in the media."

Jess didn't want them there anymore, not in her house. "But I wrote it," she said.

Alison said, "So where are your drafts? You wrote a book, but you have no copy of it or record of having sent it to anyone. Even your former agent says it's a fantasy."

Jess looked up. "Dina? You spoke to Dina?"

"She had a little holiday, and she's working for us now. Father employed her to rep the final novel."

Howard turned to Jess. He spoke ruefully. "She's set up on her own."

The lawyer picked up the briefcase from the floor and opened it on the coffee table. "As I say, there's no need for a fuss over all of this. I have documents drafted which I'd like you to take a look at." He handed them to Jess.

"It's a standard waiver, confirming you had no direct role in writing *Cleansing Soil* and relinquishing any claim on royalties. The addendum states that Mr. Stevens's estate will pay you a sum of one thousand pounds for research and support in the drafting of the novel."

Jess said, "But I wrote it."

The lawyer looked around the room at the others and stood to leave. "Have your people look it over."

* * * *

The house phone rang in the early hours. The ringing was loud and insistent, overcoming even the sleeping pills which Jess had taken earlier. When she stumbled down the stairs to the phone, the pressure on her temples was unbearable.

She picked up the phone.

"Hello?"

"Jess?"

"Dina?"

The line was grainy. Jess thought she could hear people laughing in the background. It sounded like a party. The caller said nothing in reply.

Jess spoke but her voice was weak, "You took my book."

The voice came again. "They said you were struggling. Things getting on top of you."

Jess could feel herself breaking. "You took it."

"Darling, if you continue to say these silly things, people will get worried."

"Say it, Dina. Say I wrote it."

"There was no book, Jess. That was the problem. There was never any book."

Jess's voice cracked. "But, but I thought there was."

She heard laughter in the background, then the line went dead.

* * * *

The news anchor wore a contrived smile at the corner of his lips. After the misery he'd just reported, this was the lighter, final item. A bit of culture.

"And now for the rarest of things. A genuine literary event. At midnight tonight copies of the most anticipated novel in a generation will hit the bookstores. Fans of the late author, Gerald Stevens have camped outside book shops up and down the country, awaiting the delivery of *Cleansing Soil*, said to be his masterpiece.

"To prevent leaks ahead of publication, critics were locked in secure hotel suites to read the book. The buzz created by stellar reviews has sent pre-sales through the roof. The world of publishing is ablaze with expectation.

"We're going live to the scene outside Foyles in central London where Angela Bailey is talking to two people with a special relationship to the author and this novel."

The screen cut to a female reporter, in the background rows of people stood in line.

"Thank you, David. Yes, I'm here with Alison Stevens, daughter to the late, great author, and Dina Wilmore, the agent who worked with him on this book in the final days of his life.

"Alison, this must be a bittersweet occasion for you. Your father's work is receiving both critical and popular acclaim, and yet tragically, he's not here to see it."

Alison Stevens was about to speak when Jessica turned off the television. On the coffee table in front of her was a check for one thousand pounds.

She got up from the sofa and, stepping around the clutter on the floor, started up the stairs. Jess would need more pills tonight.

Halfway up the flight, the doorbell rang. This late, Jessica wasn't expecting anyone, but so many strange things had happened recently, she thought nothing of it.

She went to the door and opened up. A delivery man stood waiting, a package in his hand.

"Sorry it's late," he said. "Special instructions."

Jess signed for the package and closed the door. She returned to the living room, the only light coming in from the streetlight outside. She sat on the chair and carefully pulled open the packaging.

Inside was a new book, *Cleansing Soil* emblazoned across the front cover and then, "Gerald Stevens." The image beneath was of a man in a field, holding a metal detector. A watercolor in the style of Lowry.

Jess opened the front cover and found a card inside, stuck to the page. The handwriting was faint and a little shaky, but unmistakably his.

> *To my dearest Jess,*
>   *Enjoy.*
>
>   *Gerald xxx*

Charlie Hughes lives in South London in the UK. He writes suspense, horror and dark psychological short stories which have been published by *Ellery Queen's Mystery Magazine*, *Mystery Weekly*, The NoSleep Podcast and various anthologies. He tweets from @charliesuspense and his website can be found at www.charliehugheswriting.blogspot.com.

THE BODYGUARD

JANICE LAW

Rein Tomaak, short and broad with a silver pompadour, was checking out a new line of motion sensors, when his office manager opened the door in a flurry of excitement. From Pat's burble of names and figures, one word emerged, *Chartreuse*.

"Who is Chartreuse?" He raised an eyebrow, for Pat, tall and lean with a clever face and thick glasses, was normally the calm center of the whole operation. He, Rein, might indulge in whimsy or temperament; Pat was all planning and forethought.

"Where have you been living? Everyone on the planet knows Chartreuse. And, Rein, it will be an excellent contract and so good for the agency. A client of the first magnitude."

"She's discovered the cure for cancer? Predicts earthquakes? Runs the UN?"

Pat made an airy, dismissive gesture. "She's a celebrity, madly famous."

"For what, exactly?"

"Well, the photos. *My Private Parts* the series was called. That was very big. It went viral. And then—"

"Sufficient unto the day," said Rein. "What does she need protection from?"

"Her fans, the world. Chartreuse literally cannot go to a store without being mobbed."

"Maybe she should have kept more things private," Rein said.

"She wants twenty-four-hour protection, including someone to accompany her driver and remain on the premises all night. Following our conversation, I ran some preliminary figures." Pat put the sheet on the desk. Rein saw that it was going to be a very profitable contract. Pat might be star struck, and it was Rein's personal opinion that her hair was on too tight, but her contracts were things of beauty.

"Denton," he suggested. "Denton and Chad and I think Marlene for night duty. That sound all right?"

"Mmmm," said Pat. "And you, of course. No, no, she asked for you by name. *I want Rein Tomaak. I want the very best.* That's what she said."

"A woman of more discernment than I credited, but I can't baby-sit some ditzy celebrity and run the office."

"A few special occasions will do, I think. Some major family gathering, that seemed to be the key thing."

"Mega celebrities have cookouts at Uncle Joe's and down a few brewskis before the ball game?"

Pat looked stunned. "You really don't know who she is?"

"Why have I been asking?"

"She's the Armiger heiress. Next in line to head the big energy conglomerate."

"And she spends her time hopping onto copiers without her foundation garments?"

"Armiger family parties," Pat said sternly, "are apt to be in the nature of corporate gatherings. I've set up a meeting for you this afternoon. Two p.m."

Rein ran a hand over his face and pursed his lips, indicating consideration and some reservations. Though he liked to think he ran a tight ship, a good deal of the rigor came from Pat, who maneuvered him very nicely. "It is a good contract," he conceded after a moment. "If she signs it."

"Signed and sealed," said Pat. "I'll call you a cab."

On the way downtown, Rein googled Chartreuse and Armiger on his iPhone, so that he was not entirely ignorant when he was deposited before a tower of blue glass and steel that shimmied up to the cloud layer. He ascended to the penthouse where a uniformed maid led him into a glass-walled room, bright with glare and overlooking a spectacular expanse of city and river.

His client was waiting for him on one of the few pieces of furniture, a free-form relative of the couch, flanked by what probably were sculptures and certainly were obscene. "Ms. Armiger, Rein Tomaak."

"Thank you for coming so soon." She motioned for him to sit down.

She was smaller than he'd expected, a tiny blonde wearing high heels, a four-inch mini-skirt, and a transparent shirt under a silk blazer. Her eyes were blue and oddly wide apart, and both her nose and lips looked to have been seriously improved.

Rein perched uncertainly on a curve of her *avant garde* sofa and checked the floor-to-ceiling views of the neighboring towers. The place was an agoraphobic's nightmare and a surveillance dream. "You are afraid," he said after a moment.

"Someone wants to kill me."

"Anyone in particular?"

"My uncle—and former legal guardian. Harden Armiger. He is presently the CEO of Armiger, Inc."

"Why would he want to do that?"

"Because when I turn twenty-five, I inherit the rest of my shares. I will become the majority shareholder, and I will control the corporation."

Rein raised his eye brows. He could see that Chartreuse, celebrity mega-star, might give corporate honchos pause. "How soon do you reach the magic number?"

"Two months," she said.

"He's left it quite late, hasn't he?"

She surprised him by laughing. "He tried, of course. But he is an amateur. And after the first time—a little 'boating accident' off the Vineyard—I've taken evasive action."

"Such as?"

"Such as stardom. Celebrity has given me protective surveillance."

Rein admitted to himself that this showed ingenuity. "So why me, why now?"

"Now is crunch time." Her face darkened. "Now he will get down to business. He will hire a professional, and I need my own expert to counter that."

"If you are serious, we need to make some changes." Rein gestured toward the vast expanse of glass and the terrace outside. "A few drapes for starters."

When she started to protest, he pointed to one of the adjacent towers. "A clear shot any time you are on your terrace. And with all this glass, your movements are easy to follow."

"All right, I can get drapes. I do shopping superlatively well."

"Now for your habits. What places do you visit often?"

"Various stores, boutiques, clubs, restaurants, art venues." She gestured expansively. "I am in demand for all sorts of special occasions."

Rein found her was an odd mixture with her diva airs and plain speech, but he launched into the security drill, cautioning her to vary her routes and to break her routine. When he thought she had grasped the essentials, he took out folders with photos and information about Denton, Chad, and Marlene. "One with you at all times. They are very experienced, well trained professionals."

"Denton looks too handsome to be professional."

"Trust me, he is," said Rein.

She studied the picture for a moment, taking in Denton's clear, even features, curly hair and guileless smile. "Don't say I didn't warn you," she giggled.

* * * *

"What's she like?" Pat asked when he got back, a question echoed by her assistant and by the computer maven and most of the staff. Clearly, Rein thought, there was a parallel universe that he had never entered.

"She's tiny," he said, "with too little clothing and too many vulgar sculptures. Also, nobody's fool. Mind yourselves." He went over the security plan with Denton, Chad, and Marlene. "The three of you can handle everything but the annual Armiger party. No lack of confidence in you and not my idea, but a key thing for her."

"Celebrities are eccentric," Marlene said, and the others nodded agreement and offered examples.

Amazing, Rein thought, that his staff should be a font of such lore. But though they were as excited as if they were guarding a head of state, Rein expected a routine case.

True, there were a couple of odd incidents: an SUV that might have hit Chartreuse outside a trendy nightspot if Denton had not been alert. Drunk driver, most likely, and when the cops ran the plate, the vehicle was reported stolen. So that was something, but Rein reserved judgment.

There was a dodgy photographer, too. One of many, as far as Rein was concerned, but when he read Marlene's report on the encounter, he was troubled. The man had followed Chartreuse from an opening for "art furniture," and Marlene had spotted something odd about the camera. She set up a ruckus and the man fled.

"I'm sure it wasn't really a camera," she said.

"A weapon of some type?" Rein asked.

"Yes, but what sort of mechanism, I don't know. Something clumsy. He kept trying to maneuver to get a clear shot."

"He would do that if he were just an ambitious paparazzi."

"Something was wrong," Marlene insisted, and Rein took that under advisement, too.

When Chartreuse called him about the Armiger party, she said, "You've read the reports. You must believe me now."

"I believed you before, but we have no proof. If we had proof, we could go to the police."

"It's called a Scots Verdict," she said. "And it's good enough for me."

* * * *

The Armiger mansion on the far reaches of Long Island was a massive brick pile with an 18th century façade dating back to when "energy provider" meant running slave ships. Big additions traced changing tastes and the family's growing respectability, ending with a glass cube that served as party central for a gathering of high flyers and beautiful people.

Rein had hired a tuxedo, and once Pat helped him with the studs and the cummerbund, he looked like a don at a Mafioso wedding. His client, on the other hand, did him proud. She wore a silver leather bustier with leather spikes over the breasts, a diamond dog collar, a silver leather mini-skirt, and five-inch silver heels. A little jeweled purse in the shape of an apple dangled from one wrist, and she took Rein's arm as she waved to the photographers.

"Don't leave me for a moment," she said.

That was the plan, and he stuck by her through canapés and cock-tails and waited patiently for her outside the ladies' powder room. "This is Rein Tomaak," she said to everyone who greeted her. "He's here to see I behave myself." Then she would laugh and lean against his shoulder, all very sex kitten and, from Rein's point of view, te-dious if not offensive. He hoped that Pat was adding a good deal of overtime to this gig.

Suddenly Chartreuse, who had been flirting and laughing and waving when she wasn't using him as a leaning post, stiffened. She'd had her hand resting on his shoulder, and he felt the muscular ten-sion as she drew herself up. "My uncle," she said, looking over her shoulder.

His features were enough like hers so that Rein might have picked him out on his own. Harden Armiger was small and slim like his niece, with angular features and blue eyes. If Chartreuse had been burdened by his knobby hawk nose, she had done well to have it altered. Harden's fair skin was deeply lined and tanned, aged beyond his years by the corporate wars and time on the water. He made Rein think of a small quick lizard, and there was something reptilian about the way he sidled up to Chartreuse and put his arm around her waist.

She stepped back. "No kiss for your old uncle?" He laughed in a nasty way. "Not even when you're wearing the family diamonds?" He laid a finger on her throat and leaned over and kissed her bare shoulder in a way that told Rein all he needed to know.

"This is Rein Tomaak," she said, her voice gone hoarse. It seemed to him that her diva airs and sophisticated control had cracked like a shell. Inside was someone he hadn't met before: someone very young and frightened. And angry. He guessed angry, too. "I've hired his security firm."

If Harden Armiger was disconcerted, he gave no sign. "Thinking ahead, my dear?" He turned to walk away.

"Always," she called after him, and though Rein could feel her shiver, she recovered herself quickly. "I must have a drink with him; I cannot look frightened; that's fatal with him."

"He doesn't seem too friendly at the moment."

"I can change that. You just watch me."

"Would you want to?"

She raised her head sharply and gave him a look. "How did you know?"

"That kiss. Plus, you've armored up for the gig. If diamond dog collars came spiked, I assume you'd have one."

"I'm not sure I like a man that astute."

"I was your special request," Rein reminded her, and when she started across the room, he moved with her.

"No, wait here for me."

"I am not to leave your side. Your stipulation."

"You'll be right in the same room. And look, there's Chad. Denton is outside on the grounds. I'm perfectly safe." She pressed his arm and added, "You're very kind. I'm not used to that."

She strode toward where her uncle was standing with some friends. Rein saw her lift a couple flutes of champagne from a passing waiter. Then she was lost for a moment in the crowd, and he had just enough time to feel anxious before she reached her uncle and handed him a glass.

He was too far away to hear anything over the hubbub, but Rein saw him raise his glass. Then she leaned toward her uncle and whispered something in his ear. He laid a hand on her silver haunch and laughed.

A few minutes later, Chartreuse was back, very bright, very up. She stood swaying from one foot to the other. "Do you dance?" she asked.

"Strictly ballroom."

She put out her hand. "This is a rumba." When he looked surprised, she said, "I was raised with all the airs and graces."

So Rein, who was light footed and easy moving, got out on the floor. Soon he and Chartreuse were doing fancy moves and cameras were flashing. They only stopped for more flutes of champagne and a brief visit to the powder room, where Chartreuse, true to her word, was "only a minute."

Back with the band, they assayed a mamba. Having kicked off the crippling heels, Chartreuse was showing an admirable turn of foot, when Rein noticed that Harden Armiger had abandoned his corporate buddies for points unknown. Suddenly there was, not a commotion, nothing as definite as that, but a fast-moving security man, a hurried conference, and a sudden alteration in the atmosphere that Rein detected despite a good Latin beat and more champagne than was prudent.

"Stop," he said to Chartreuse. "Something's happened." He took her arm and hustled across to the French doors onto the terrace.

He heard an ambulance, then Denton appeared at his elbow, whispering, "Something's happened to Harden Armiger. Out by the summer house."

Chartreuse turned dead white; she would have fallen if Denton hadn't grabbed her. Half an hour later the estate was crawling with police, and an ambulance had removed the blanketed corpse of Chartreuse's uncle, who had fallen into the handsome lily pond and drowned.

* * * *

Of course there was an investigation which, like so many, raised almost as many questions as it answered. Harden Armiger had alcohol in his blood stream. A good deal, in fact, but as Chartreuse told the investigators, her uncle operated on alcohol as a normal thing. Also cocaine, not entirely unexpected, either, and Rohypnol, which was a surprise.

"Anxiety," Chartreuse remarked. "It is legitimately prescribed for anxiety." Though what Harden Armiger had to be anxious about was left uncertain.

There was speculation, some of it unkind, a big funeral, and a full-page tribute ad in the *Times*, paid for by Armiger, Inc. Rein got a large check for his efforts. This was some consolation for the loss of Denton, who had gone on leave a week after the inquest and subsequently emailed that he "had some things to sort out and wouldn't be returning to the agency."

Rein felt uneasy about that, and his anxiety only increased when he got a very formal letter on Armiger, Inc. stationary, requesting his presence at Armiger headquarters. "We are interested in a new security arrangement and would like to speak with you about a contract." It was signed Chartreuse Armiger, for the board of directors.

Although Pat was thrilled, Rein felt surly, but he was curious enough to visit a corner office in the company's soaring steel and glass slab. Chartreuse was waiting for him behind a desk as big as a tanker. She told her secretary to hold her calls, and she stood up and extended her hand to Rein.

He was no fashionista, but he couldn't miss the change. She was dressed in a black suit with a fitted jacket over a white blouse and a long black skirt. She still had the five-inch heels but otherwise she was strictly formal and strictly business.

Chartreuse noticed his glance. "Corporate mourning."

"And are you—mourning?"

"Hardly," she said. "You saw what he was."

Rein nodded and sat down.

"I propose that your firm take over Armiger security." She outlined the parameters of a job that would have sent Pat into ecstasy. "It would mean a large expansion," she concluded, "but we could ensure you'd have access to the needed capital."

Rein shook his head and felt sad. Sad for Pat, sad for Denton. "Impossible," he said. "And unwise."

"Why?"

"You used me as your alibi, and you corrupted Denton. I lost a good employee."

"I did warn you that he was too handsome."

"He killed your uncle at worst, ignored his accident at best."

"Accident, surely," she said quickly.

"Surely? I would like to know what you were carrying in that little purse and what you told your uncle that you made sure I wouldn't hear."

Chartreuse said nothing.

"I'm guessing you invited him to the summer house. Then you had that quick visit to the powder room. He was gone after that. He thought you had given me the slip and gone to meet him."

She shrugged. "He had no idea what he'd done to my life. Not the slightest."

"It's easy to be careless when you are very rich."

"What's that supposed to mean?"

"Denton's off 'finding himself.' Losing himself somewhere without extradition is my translation."

"The coroner, the inquest, all those investigating officers found for accident, didn't they?"

"It was carefully done, but had it failed, my reputation and my firm might have been ruined—all to provide you with a backup alibi."

"I was in danger," she said quickly, her face white against her brilliant lipstick and her vivid eyes.

"Were you? Your uncle was a pedophile but not necessarily a killer. My guess is that he thought he could control you even as an adult. He didn't see how much you resemble him or how fond you are of power."

She was silent for a moment before she asked, "What are you going to do?"

Rein stood up. "I have no proof but I'm not going to be complicit."

"I could have trusted you," she said with what seemed like genuine regret, and when they reached the door of her office, she shook his hand. "I will think of you when I hear a dance band."

Her expression was so wistful, that Rein softened a trifle. "When they play a rumba," he suggested and let himself out.

✗

Janice Law is an Edgar-nominated and a Lambda-award-winning novelist, as well as short fiction writer whose most recent stories have appeared in *Alfred Hitchcock's Mystery Magazine*, *Ellery Queen's Mystery Magazine*, and *Sherlock Holmes Mystery Magazine*. Her most recent novels are *Mornings in London* (mysteriouspress.com), and *Homeward Dove* (Wildside Press). Visit her at www.janicelaw.com.

TRIGGER WARNING

DENNIS PALUMBO

Though the flight attendant knew that U.S. Air Marshalls carry weapons while flying, she still gave my gun a wary look. I hadn't realized my jacket had opened, revealing the belt holster. I quickly re-buttoned it.

The pilot must have tipped her off about who I was, since, like all my colleagues, I was in plain, nondescript clothes. Which, in general, is a pretty fair description of myself.

I sat back in my seat. After changing planes in Denver, it was a short flight to northwest Montana, whose dense forests and glacier-spawned mountains spread to the horizon in the view through my window.

She bent to follow my gaze over my shoulder. "Is this your first time here?" she asked.

"Yes."

"Then you're in for a treat. How long are you staying?"

"As long as it takes."

This brought a brief, curious frown, after which she moved briskly down the aisle. Minutes later, we began our descent.

The five-hour journey from Cleveland, which had begun just before noon, ended at Kalispell Airport. Travelling without luggage, I deplaned, stopped at an outlet kiosk, and then found a car rental stall. Selecting a Jeep four-wheeler, I signed for it with one of the other ID's I use. Prompts less questions from the guy behind the desk.

I was on the road heading south by late afternoon, relishing the endless breadth of my surroundings, especially after the cramped seating on both planes. The sun was bright and welcoming, the aspens and grasslands on either side of the road were lush, and I even caught sight of a mule deer grazing near the foothills. But for an urban boy like me, it was the expanse of clear, startling blue overhead that dazzled. No wonder Montana was called Big Sky Country.

Following the signs, I drove to Flathead Lake, at whose eastern edge was the small town of Praiswater. The lakeside community was barely a dot on the map, but it was where Andy Hackett had chosen to retire. Far away from his old job, and his old life.

But not quite far enough.

* * * *

According to Google, Flathead Lake is the largest fresh-water lake west of the Mississippi, spanning 188 square miles of pristine water. I could believe it, as I drove on and on along its curving, tree-trimmed shoreline, squinting in the sun for any sign of Praiswater.

An *actual* sign would help, I thought, my city-slicker frustration growing.

It was just dusk when I finally spotted the turn-off and headed down a narrow, rutted road shrouded by the interlocking foliage of a tree canopy.

Following a smaller access road, its sides flanked by some size-able apple and pear orchards, I entered what I assumed was Praiswater proper. A modest town square, ringed by hedges interspersed with the occasional plum tree. And, just beyond, a small diner, grocery store, gas station and red-bricked postal annex. No doubt where the locals kept their P.O. boxes.

I pulled to the curb in front of a large, wood-framed building, over whose front doors were the words "Praiswater Fishing Tackle and Supplies." I slipped out of my jacket and pulled on the grey hood-ie and cap I'd bought at the airport. Hood up, cap down, dark glasses on. I went in.

The guy standing behind the service counter wore a full beard, with leathery skin and wind-whipped eyes. His name tag read "Phil." There was also a Navy service pin on the lapel

of his flannel shirt. A veteran. Iraq or Iran, I guessed, considering his age.

"Help ya, mister?" The predictable suspicious squint.

"Hope so. I'm looking for Andy Hackett's place."

I took out my cell and showed him the address she'd sent me in her last text. "I have his address right here. But I don't see any signs for Orchard Lane, and—"

"You a friend o' his?"

"Sort of. We met some years ago, and I thought I'd look him up again."

"What's your business with ol' Andy, anyway? He didn't say nothin' 'bout expectin' company."

"Let's just say it's a surprise."

"Uh-huh." Phil tugged on his scraggly beard. "Truth is, I don't think Andy cares much for surprises. Kinda keeps to himself. Him and the wife."

A long, thick silence followed.

"Sure you're friends with Andy?" he said at last.

"Like I said, from a long time ago."

He paused, then nodded at a young couple who'd just entered the store. "Look, mister, I got a business to run. So if you ain't buyin' nothin', I got *real* customers need waitin' on…"

I held up a palm. "No problem. If you could just tell me the best way to get to Orchard Lane—"

Grunting, he pointed past me through the front window. I turned to look. In the fading light, I could just make out a slim woman with short dark hair climbing into the cab of a flatbed truck. A bag of groceries under one arm.

"Best way?" he said. "I'd probably follow that lady there. She's Andy's wife, Diane, and looks like she's headin' home."

It was weird. Even from this distance, and after all these years, I still recognized her. I'd wondered if I would.

* * * *

I followed her to an isolated spot ten miles out of town, obscured within a dense clutch of overgrown trees. I parked about a hundred yards from the Hackett cottage, a sturdily-built place with a peaked roof and whitewashed wood, my rental safely hidden between two leafy conifers. From my vantage point, I could see Diane slide easily out of the truck and carry her groceries inside the house.

I hurriedly removed my hoodie, cap and sunglasses. Donned again my off-the-rack sports jacket. No sense appearing more threatening than necessary.

Climbing out of the Jeep, I crossed the semi-circle gravel girding the front of the cottage. I was just about to step up onto the porch when I heard a voice. Male.

"Stop right there, bucko."

Calling from within the house. From the open window to my right. A belligerent, alcohol-fueled voice.

I turned to see that the window curtain had been pushed back, the nose of a rifle sticking out. Wavering a little in its owner's drunken grasp.

I raised my hands. "I'm unarmed," I lied.

"Then you're a bigger fool than I thought."

"That may be. But I'm also a Federal agent, so I wouldn't be waving that gun in my face if I were you."

Suddenly the front door swung open, Diane's handsome features somewhat hidden behind the glare of the twin porch lights that had just come on. But I could see the corners of her mouth turn up slightly. A weary bemusement.

Without shifting her gaze from mine, she called out to the man holding the rifle.

"It's okay, hon. Put that thing away, all right?"

After a long moment, I saw the rifle barrel slowly withdraw. The window closed, the curtain falling into place.

I turned back to the woman in front of me. She'd cut her long hair, wearing it in a kind of bob. And her lined face indicated a strain not wholly due to the passage of time. But her eyes were the same. Dark brown. Sharp. Grave.

She leaned in to me. "I have the money," she whispered.

I said nothing. Diane held the door open and I went in.

* * * *

She led me into the pinewood-paneled main room, whose two cushioned chairs and leather couch were angled toward a huge bricked-in fireplace. Some Charles Marion Russell prints and a faux Native American throw rug completed the Old West motif.

It was a masculine room, in the most stereotypic sense, so it seemed only fitting that one of the chairs would be occupied by a stout, big-bellied man in jeans and cowboy boots, holding a beer. A boozy scowl carved a line in his heavy, sunburned jowls. That same rifle, a Remington, lay across his knees.

"Who the hell are you?" Rheumy eyes blinking, trying to focus.

"Ben Walker." The name was one of my favorites.

Diane spoke up. "He's an old friend. From college. He let me know he was passing through, so I invited him to visit."

He grunted his displeasure. Ignoring him, Diane motioned me to the chair opposite where her husband sat. I took it.

Hackett looked up at her. "Get me another beer, will ya, Di? For Walker here, too, I guess." He shifted uncomfortably in his seat. "A quick snort, okay, pal? One for the road."

"Sure. I'll make it quick."

Diane moved across the room and through an opened door that presumably led to the kitchen. Which left me and Hackett alone.

"So… you're some kinda Fed?"

"U.S. Air Marshall."

"Cops are cops, ya want my opinion. Don't matter what kinda badge ya got."

Hackett laughed hoarsely. "I mean, hell, I had me a number o' run-ins with cops back in the day. I ran a construction outfit, and there was always some bullshit 'bout…" Voice slurred, hesitant. "What was it? Oh, yeah, crap 'bout inferior materials. Work not up to code. Gave me all kinds o' grief."

He shook his head, then finished his beer. I'd already noticed the four bottles on the floor next to Hackett's chair.

Just then, Diane returned with two fresh bottles, handing one each to Hackett and me. Her eyes held mine.

"Andy left out the part about skipping town, right before the warrants showed up." She sighed. "Being married to a fugitive was a ton of fun. For better or worse, right, hon?"

Hackett waved his hand dismissively. "That was years ago, Diane. Cops got better things to do now. Nobody cares 'bout an old bastard like me no more."

Diane sat stiffly on the couch. Ever since we'd entered the room, her movements had been measured, careful. As though it was taking a great effort to hold herself together.

Under the circumstances, I can't say I blamed her.

"Water under the bridge…" Hackett took another satisfying pull on his beer. "How'd you two meet, anyway?"

Diane managed a smile. "Like I said, in college. Back east. We were together for quite a—"

Her husband's eyes narrowed, steely with malice. "So you weren't exactly just friends, eh?"

My own eyes stayed riveted on that rifle still cradled on his knees. His fat fingers stroking the wooden stock.

Her voice grew firm. "No, Andy, we weren't. Truth is, we were in love. After a couple of years, we even started talking about marriage. Kids."

"Ya don't say?"

I let my gaze drift up to meet his. "Don't sweat it, Andy. Diane couldn't go through with it. Left town without saying good-bye." I shrugged. "She kinda broke my heart."

This brought another hoarse, hollow laugh from Hackett. Then he looked at Diane.

"You did that, sweetie? Just off-loaded the poor bastard? *Now* who's the one who skipped town? Christ, you bitches are all the same."

With that, he drained his beer. Hand shaking as he reached to place the bottle next to its brethren on the floor. It slipped from his fingers and rolled under the chair.

Ignoring him, Diane turned to face me. "I'm sorry. That was a terrible thing to do to you. But you know how hard decisions were for me. Remember when I wanted to go to Paris for my sophomore year but chickened out at the last minute? Just like I wanted to marry you—I *really* did—but when the time came, somehow I couldn't. I was always like that. My dad used to make fun of me about it. He used to say, 'Diane, you just can't pull the trigger.' Guess he was right."

With a drunken chuckle, Hackett waved a shaky finger at me.

"See, buddy? No need to feel bad. *I'm* the one been stuck with her since then. Talk about bad decisions…"

By now his eyelids had begun to droop, his fleshy jowls falling to his chest. He tried to jerk himself awake.

"All these years o' goddam wedded bliss… Yeah, right…" Words now a breathy, angry whisper. Mere puffs of air.

Diane and I exchanged guarded looks.

In less than a minute, Hackett had drifted into a drunken stupor. A deep, sloppy sleep.

The rifle slipped from his lap to the floor.

By now, I'd pulled on my gloves, so it was safe to pick it up. The only prints on it would be his.

Diane let out a long, grateful breath.

"You see what he's like?" Her gaze never leaving Hackett's sleeping form, his shoulders rising and falling. "It's been like this for years. The drinking. The physical and verbal abuse. And sex with him? It was like being with a rutting pig."

She shivered briefly at the memory.

"I always wondered what had happened to you," I said, holding the rifle loosely at my side. "Then hearing from you last week. After all this time."

She nodded. "I know. It was… crazy, I guess. But I was desperate. Needed help. Then I thought of you. How much we'd loved each other back then. How special I thought you were. Though I admit I was kinda surprised when I looked you up and—"

"Yeah. Been an Air Marshall for a couple years now."

Diane leaned back on the couch. "Funny, but when I saw that, it occurred to me that you might be willing to help me out. If not for old times' sake, then for the money… You can't be making much as a Fed. Not if you're living as well as you used to say you wanted to. You had a lot of big dreams, the kind that don't come true on an Air Marshall's salary."

"You're right. That's why I do a little moonlighting once in a while. To supplement the income."

At the mention of money, we exchanged another meaningful look. Then, with a rueful smile, she hurried off, to return a minute or two later with an envelope. She handed it to me.

"Ten thousand, as agreed." She sniffed.

I didn't even look inside, but just stuffed it in my back pocket. Then I moved closer to Hackett's sleeping form and knelt in front of his chair.

"Ready?" I said to her.

Diane paled. "I— I don't have to be here, do I? Jesus, I don't want to see—"

"Strange, since it was your idea. To make it look like a suicide. He's drunk, depressed, can't go on…"

"I know, but… I mean, I've imagined it a hundred times. Seen myself, in my mind, actually positioning the rifle. But now I…"

"You can't pull the trigger. Yeah, I got that."

She must have heard something in my voice that brought the stinging color back to her face. Then, without another word, she hurried from the room.

The first thing I did was take off my shoes and walk with them toward the front door. Opening it, I placed them on the wicker welcome mat. Then it was back to the main room.

Once I had the Remington's butt end placed on the floor, all I had to do was wedge the rifle up between Hackett's fat thighs, the barrel end shoved under his chin. Careful not to wake him—though I doubt anything could at this point—I curled his forefinger around the trigger, my gloved finger over it.

And squeezed.

The shot sounded like a cannon's roar, reverberating in the room. Hackett's face split, blood and brains exploding upwards, spraying the wall behind him. Spattering one of the prints.

A fair amount got on me, too. But I could deal with that soon enough. Any blood splatter on the floor or elsewhere would be accounted for by the severity of the wound. As long as I didn't track it anywhere.

In my socks, I stepped carefully back from the slow-welling pool, formed by rivulets draining from Hackett's shattered head.

By then, Diane had dared to peek around the opened door to the kitchen to see things for herself. Face gone white again, eyes round as black poker chips, she could only stare.

I joined her at the door. Her eyes now pinched, anxious.

"What do I do now? Call the police? Or maybe go away, let someone else find him…?"

"Won't matter." I cocked the rifle.

"What do you mean?"

"It'll look like a domestic gone sideways. Andy gets drunk, grabs his rifle, shoots you. Then, stricken with remorse, kills himself. Cops'll buy it. They've seen it often enough."

Diane stared, breathless, uncomprehending. Until the realization slowly dawned…

"But— but why? I've *paid* you, for Christ's sake—!"

"Yes. And I appreciate it. Been a slow month."

Her hand reached out to clutch my arm. I shook it off.

"But we… we loved each other once, remember? I *still* love you… With him dead, we can go away… anywhere you want…"

"We *could*, yeah… but I have some serious trust issues where you're concerned. Besides, a pro never leaves loose ends."

"A— a pro? What do you mean?"

I shrugged. "You were right about the limits of a marshall's salary. That's why I had to pick a second career. Quite a lucrative one at that."

Her mouth opened, but no sounds came out.

"Besides, if it's any consolation, you got my services for way below my usual fee. A bargain, in fact."

I took two steps back and fired.

* * * *

As luck would have it, I found myself served by that same flight attendant on the ride back home. We chatted amiably for a few minutes, even joked about the service weapon still strapped in my holster. Then she went off to see to other passengers.

Good looking girl, I thought. Maybe I'll ask for her number when we land.

I closed my eyes and let my head fall back against the seat rest. I had to admit, it was a pretty sweet set-up. Convenient as hell. A U.S. Marshall can fly anywhere while carrying a gun.

It was like the old TV show: Have gun, will travel.

Yep, pretty sweet set-up for a hit man. Or contract killer. Or whatever the hell the term is nowadays.

Of course, after killing Diane, I returned the rifle to Hackett's dead hands, careful to avoid stepping in the blood. Then I closed the front door behind me, wiped the handle of any prints, put my shoes back on and got in the Jeep.

On my way back to town, I got rid of my burner cell, as well as the hoodie, cap and sunglasses. Then I pulled into a rest stop, stripped out of my blood-spattered clothes, and dressed in the ones I'd also bought at the outlet kiosk. I shoved the dirty clothes into a trash can and found my way back to the highway.

I wasn't worried about Phil, back at the Praiswater fishing supplies store. If questioned about any strangers in town, all he could describe was a guy whose face was hidden under a cloth hood and cap, and behind dark glasses.

When I reached the airport, I left the Jeep at the rental agency's parking lot. No need to wipe the steering wheel, or anything else inside, since I'd always worn gloves when driving.

Plus, since both the ID and credit card I'd used to rent the Jeep were stolen, I couldn't be traced that way, either.

Just then, the pretty flight attendant came by again, offering fresh coffee. I took a cup and gingerly sipped the hot brew, watching her tempting rear end as she sidled off.

Then, to my surprise, my mind went again to the look on poor Diane's face right before I shot her in the heart. Nice metaphor, actually, since that's what she'd done to me, all those years ago.

Right in the heart.

Well, maybe not shot it, but certainly chilled it. Turned it to ice. Been that way ever since.

So it was with mixed feelings that I got her phone call last week. Her pleas for my help. Her offer of money. She even had a plan. A way to make it look like suicide.

But she couldn't do it herself. That's why she needed me.
She couldn't pull the trigger, she'd said.
Turns out, I always can.

✗

Formerly a Hollywood screenwriter (*My Favorite Year*; *Welcome Back, Kotter*, etc.), Dennis Palumbo is a licensed psychotherapist and author. His mystery fiction has appeared in *Ellery Queen's Mystery Magazine*, *The Strand* and elsewhere, and is collected in *From Crime to Crime* (Tallfellow Press). His series of mystery thrillers (*Mirror Image, Fever Dream, Night Terrors, Phantom Limb*, and the latest, *Head Wounds*, which was named *Suspense Magazine*'s "Best of 2018") feature Daniel Rinaldi, a psychologist and trauma expert who consults with the Pittsburgh Police. For more info, visit www.dennispalumbo.com.

BLUE SKIES
KEITH SNYDER

A stubby concrete shed broke the line of the chain-link perimeter fence. The fence was threaded with privacy slats and draped with tarps. There were faint keypad beeps in the shed, and then the metal door was shoved open from the inside. The man who'd shoved it was Tom Krol.

The dark-haired man who'd buzzed was wearing a red flowered shirt. He had a big nose. He held up a printout. "Let's see those excavators."

Krol pointed at a thick white envelope in the man's breast pocket. "Let's see the money."

The visitor said, "Not out here."

* * * *

The shed wasn't a yard office, just an entry point. Bare concrete, a grate floor, and perforated metal stairs going down. At the bottom, it was fifteen degrees cooler and the floor was concrete. A recliner and sofa squared at the edges of a fringed rug. The ceiling was corrugated metal, with a welded seam crossing its ribs.

Krol turned at the bottom. "Let's see the cash."

"Shouldn't you search me for recording devices?"

Krol smiled a little. "If that's what you're into." The patdown was authoritative and unpracticed. The visitor held the envelope and the printout in his raised hands and looked at the room. Behind the sofa were a couple of wooden pallets stacked with boxes of ammunition and freeze-dried food, five-gallon tubs of honey, and jumbo cans of coffee. To the right of these, set back behind a thin counter and two stools, was a molded plastic mini-sink that would fit in a boat or RV. To the left, behind the recliner and metal shelving unit with more supplies on it, was a door. A framed black-and-white photo hung next to it. The photo was of two girls around nine and five years old and a woman behind them whose head had been cropped off. The woman's hands were crossed loosely in front of the girls.

Krol finished and stepped away. "Feel safer now?"

"I felt pretty safe already." The visitor put the envelope back in his shirt pocket.

"Let's see the money."

"If we reach a deal, I'll get it."

Krol's look said *really*.

"You must be used to that," the visitor said.

"Yeah. Okay. All right. That's fine. Let's go show you the goods."

"So give me the background."

Krol stopped. "The background."

"Pedigree. What I'm buying."

"Two excavators for a third what they're worth, plus paperwork. You know what you're buying."

"Who's looking for them?"

"Nobody's looking for them."

"Then why are you letting them go for a third what they're worth?"

Krol smiled. "Don't worry about that."

"I'd like to see that paperwork."

"Let's look at the machines. If you don't like them, paperwork doesn't matter."

"I'm sure they're fine." The visitor looked around, took in the place, nodded. "Let's talk about your ad."

Krol pointed at the paper still in the visitor's hand. "Two excavators, a hundred grand. What's to talk about?"

"Oh." The visitor looked at the paper. "Not that ad." He flipped it over. The other side also had printing. "This ad. *Make my ex-wife disappear*, five K, and an anonymized email address."

Krol's impatience didn't go away, but he became very still.

The visitor said, "I don't care about your earth movers."

Krol's body shifted slightly. The visitor said, "You don't need a weapon." He spread his arms. "Search me again if you want."

"Who are you? Why'd you pretend you were here about the machines?"

"I get to see more that way. With this kind of ad?" The visitor displayed the paper so the ex-wife ad showed. "We meet in a parking lot, you're jumpy, you think I'm recording you, I don't get a sense of you, it's all very tense." He flipped the paper over. "But with this kind?" He pointed around the space. "You're a prepper. Those are your kids.

That's where you stash your gun. Plus, now you're wondering how I connected the person who posted *this* ad with the person who posted *this* ad, since you thought they were both anonymous. You wanting the answer could work to my advantage."

"Who are you?"

"Let's start at the beginning."

"Let's start with your name."

"You don't find out my name. I leave here, I'm in the wind." The visitor smiled suddenly. "You're thinking *If you leave here*. And who knows? Nothing's for certain."

"What do you want?"

"To answer this ad."

"You're going to make my ex-wife disappear."

"After I walk out, Ruby Anita Charles vanishes from your life."

Krol's face went dead.

The visitor said, "I'm trying to impress you with my level of pre-paredness. Too much?"

"Who the fuck are you?"

"I'm not going to tell you."

"Maybe I'll just beat it out of you."

The visitor let a few seconds pass.

"That won't go the same as when you do it to a woman," he said.

Krol's dead stare didn't change. The visitor said, "Six CV nine eight nine five five oh seven three. That's the number of a restraining order against Thomas Rudolph Krol."

"Uh huh."

The visitor waved a hand. "Anybody who can type your name and pay twenty bucks gets that number. The impressive part is I knew what name to type. How'd I get that from two anonymous ads?"

Krol's expression was still dead, but his color had risen.

"I'm here to present a solution to you."

"Got all the solutions I need."

"Five K to someone who answers an ad on the darkweb?" He shook his head. "You're smarter than that."

"So you've got something better. Just not for five K."

"You'll be happy to pay ten times that much."

The dead stare relaxed. A few smile lines came out. "You're here to blackmail me."

"Locked in down here with you and whatever guns you've got stashed around? I'd be the world's deadest blackmailer. Let me just lay this out for you. It kind of has to go in a certain order, or it won't make sense."

Krol leaned smoothly toward the metal shelves and came out with a revolver dangling from his hand. Keeping an eye on the visitor, he went to the mini-sink, waited for a glass to fill from the thin-necked tap, drank it, carefully set down the glass, turned back, and said, "Okay, spill it."

The visitor gestured at the hanging gun. "I'm that threatening?"

In a moment, Krol smiled, cocked the gun, and put it on the tiny counter.

"All right. There are several problems that get solved by what I want to lay out for you today. Let's start with the one you said you wanted: Make your ex-wife disappear. If you google *how much does it cost to kill someone*, there's a common figure. Five grand, right? So you figure, okay, that's the going rate. And it is. ATF uses it all the time when they pretend to be low-end hit men."

"Is that what you charge?"

"I'm not ATF. Or a hit man. Now, the first thing you need to understand is this: It's never gonna be five grand."

"If you're not—"

The visitor put up a hand. "I know the questions. I need to present this all in order. So you meet this five-grand guy you found on the Internet. Thirty percent chance he's ATF, and boom, you're arrested. Figure fifty for lawyers, *plus* six figures in fines, *plus* this business you've built up takes a major hit, *plus* even if there's no prison time?" He pointed at the ammunition and the tubs of honey. "You used to be a guy off the grid, but not anymore. Nothing puts you on the grid, with Christmas tree lights, like a Federal trial."

"Thirty percent chance he's ATF."

"Right, I agree. That means seventy percent he's not. So let's say that's how it goes down. He's not."

"Terrific.

"Let's say I leave here and you think, nameless guy's got a point. I'm gonna be smart, go higher than five, find myself a *reputable* assassin. So you google some more. The next price point looks like twenty. And hey—you find a guy. Solid references, takes the twenty, doesn't blackmail you, week later she's gone."

"Great."

"But notice—I said it wouldn't be five, and it's not."

"Twenty's fine."

"It's not going to be twenty, either. It's going to be twenty—*plus*."

"Okay, I'll bite. Plus what."

"Buckle up." At Krol's look, he smiled. "Okay. Say she vanishes. No blood, no hair, no body, no email, no witness, nothing. Just—poof. Even if that all goes perfect? Because twenty-grand guy is a criminal wizard? Guess what. Tom Krol is immediately the prime suspect anyway. Because he's her ex. But it's not going to go perfect. This isn't some elite movie assassin. Of course he leaves fingerprints, or casings, or he snags her sweater, or the neighbor knocks, or the car gets rear-ended, or, or, or. Or maybe twenty-grand guy really is smart, so he subcontracts it to ten-grand guy, and *that* guy's an idiot. Plus, what if instead of killing her, he blackmails you? Or *after* he kills her?"

"He'd implicate himself."

"Only if he's a moron. All he's got to do is cut himself out of a video and send it to the cops."

"That's not admissible."

"Who cares? That just means they can't use it in court. It's still the handle on a zipper. Cops get their fingers on the handle, pull it, see what pops out. That's you. You're what pops out. So prime suspect, back on the grid, the whole salami."

"Or maybe none of that happens."

"This man of sterling character whacks your ex-wife and life goes back to normal?" The visitor nodded seriously. "Sure, that could happen." He pointed his chin at the picture of the two girls. "I assume that's Jody Michelle, now age fifteen, and Irene Louise, now age eleven? If mom's dead, guess who gets to pay for everything."

"I already pay for everything."

The visitor looked as though he was sorting through responses.

"No, you don't," he said.

Krol's eyes flicked away briefly. "She's the one who didn't want child support."

"Yeah. All right. The point is, there's no world where it's twenty grand and out. The kids' upkeep alone is six figures over the next decade. Do the math. I did." He laughed. "Plus it's just kinda rich how she's dead, but she's still squeezing you for cash."

"Yeah," Krol said, flatly. "That would be Ruby."

"Plus, did you know they bill you for prosecuting you these days? Oh yeah, you get to pay for that now. Brings the running total up to a few hundred grand. Plus let's not forget your girls are watching dad try to prove he didn't kill mom, which he did. There's no unfucking their minds from that. Therapy, school psychologist, CPS...." He waved his hands. "But I got off-topic there. We haven't gotten into the real numbers yet."

"The girls will be fine."

The visitor glanced at the picture, looked at Krol.

"Yeah," he said. "So also. Guess what else! You're a news story. *Area Prepper Buys Hit On Wife.*"

"Ex-wife."

"Sure. But hey. Maybe none of this happens! Cops don't care she's dead, neighbors aren't acting weird around you, media moves on, kids are cool you had their mom shot, doing great in school, love their daddy, everything's exactly like it was—only nicer! Because she's dead! That could happen. Everybody could just—forget!" He finished with the pleasure of a man who's been presented with an unexpected gift.

Krol didn't respond.

"Don't worry, we're into the next part of the presentation now. But you know who doesn't forget? Here's a letter you get one day. Dear Sir. How you doing? Saw you on the news. Funny thing, we don't have any tax returns from you since the Reagan days. Remit them, would you please? Love, your new BFFs at the Internal Revenue Service. And hey, looks like you lit up the state tax radar too. They're less friendly than the IRS. Dear asshole, it's eleven fifty-nine, you got 'til noon, pay up. And realize, now, this isn't just back taxes. It's back taxes, Federal. Back taxes, state. Penalties and interest, Federal. Penalties and interest, state. They will dig into you like you've never been dug before. These guys go up your ass looking for gold fillings and pull them out the same way. Which brings your losses up to what now? Two million? Three?" He put his fingers to his chest. "For my purposes, I estimated conservatively at one point four. Now, I have no doubt you have stashes I could never uncover. But *they* will. They'll pry the lid off everything you've got buried." He pointed at the seamed metal ceiling. "Not a metaphor. They won't even have to bring in their own earth movers."

"That it?"

"No. It's a good stopping point for questions, though."

"You got a whole lot of *ifs* in there. *If* the IRS watches the news. *If* I light up the state tax system. If, if, if, if, if."

"Sure, it's a crapshoot which of those things will happen. But it's never going to resemble five grand, not twenty, not even two hundred.

It could cost you everything, and probably will. And people *won't* forget, the cops *will* be looking, your kids *will* talk. The question is, what's a better way?"

"Why do I think you've got one? Though not for five grand."

"What kind of idiot would ask five grand to get you out of a seven-figure loss?"

Krol smiled. "I see. How much?"

"Can I lay out the pitch?"

"My daughters won't talk."

"Pardon?"

"They're obedient. They're good little girls. They do exactly what I tell them to do, and nothing I tell them not to."

The visitor's face was unreadable. "Got it." He pursed his lips. "So. Next thing. Why I'm here. And that is, when you get what you want, I get what I want."

"Great."

"Now, let's talk about the chain of events that brought us together. Back up, review a little history. There's this guy, Tom Krol. He's very smart."

"Don't you forget it."

"Oh, I don't. He's got a one-man operation pretty well together. Does this, does that, buys and sells things…. An unclaimed shipping container, some narcotics, file some serial numbers off some guns, move a few stolen cars. He's good at it. But he's got a problem. He wants to get bigger, but he's already doing as much as one man can do. So either he has to bring in more people, which also brings new risk, or keep the one-man operation and start moving a different variety of merchandise that's more profitable per-unit."

"This is a terrific story."

"It's a common bind. He likes Option B better—something he already knows how to do, only bigger profit. Not narcotics, too dangerous. But some rich new vein, where he can become a recognized brand. The guy everyone goes to for X, whatever X is. He's not that slick with computers, but he does manage to download Tor and poke around on the darkweb, and he bumps into something that, you know? Maybe could be X. Backhoes, excavators…. Heavy construction equipment. Bigger than cars, harder to hide—but the serial number and anti-theft stuff are pretty primitive. So yeah. This could be it. He'll need bigger covered hiding places, though." He pointed up at an angle, behind Krol. "New greenhouses."

"Vertical farming."

"Oh, sure. Preppers need broccoli. So things actually go well. He moves a few pieces. At least one was a grader he bought at auction for more than he could ever turn it around for. But that's fine—he doesn't need a profit on every deal, he just needs to learn the territory. And then, at some point, it's time to ramp it up. Which equals multi-unit orders. A forklift and a skid-steer, maybe a couple track-loaders. But with those bigger orders come clients who want deniability. They want to be able to say they were deceived. I thought it was a legal purchase! Here's the paperwork! What? It's forged?"

He waited for a response, then continued.

"But the reality is, those forged papers are probably never being put to the test. Nobody's looking all that hard for stolen earth movers. All law enforcement is gonna do is key the number into LoJack and see if anything pings. Probably nothing does, so they're done. Nobody's asking your buyer for paperwork. It's just a psychological prop to help make the sale. But even so, they still want it." He nodded. "But—this guy Tom can't do the computer stuff for the forging. So who can? He doesn't want to use outside people—he's trying to keep everything in-house. But again—he's smart. He does exactly what he should. Identifies a weakness, identifies a resource, and brings the two together."

He left space for a response. Krol waited back at him.

"And the resource he brings in? Is perfect. No record, loyal, hard to prosecute. No kidding. Well done. And the price is certainly right."

Again, Krol didn't respond.

"So—you're off. And pretty soon, luck meets preparedness. Somebody on the darkweb wants a backhoe, two excavators, and a couple of skip loaders, with papers, two hundred grand cash for the set. And this is perfect—because...." He counted on his fingers. "You know where to get a backhoe, a pair of excavators is about to go up for auction in Ohio, and skip loaders are like hookers, you just drive around at night and pick one up. So you answer the ad. *I'm your man, I'm gonna deliver!* Buyer says prove it. So all right! Off to the races! You grab your flatbed and your forger and you go to Ohio to *get those excavators!*" He clucked slightly. "Which is the first thing you did that wasn't smart."

Krol was looking coolly interested.

The visitor smiled and continued. "Now. Either you didn't realize you'd be bidding on a couple of very nice Volvos, or you didn't know how high the bidding would go—or how fast. Client's paying you two hundred grand for all five pieces? Bidding on the Volvos hits that number in about a minute, and it's still going like a rocket. Smart move is pull the plug, let them go. But you already went and acted like a big shot with the client. Two-ten, two-twenty. You gotta do something. Two-twenty-five. Two-thirty. What do you do now? Well, you do what smart, unprepared people always do. You pull out a wild card, and you throw it down, boom. You turn to your forger and say tell that guy I'll give him ten grand to stop bidding."

Krol scratched his upper lip, not breaking his interested gaze.

"Reckless," the visitor said. "And now your forger's frozen up and doesn't know what to do. But you get right down in her face, and she unfreezes and does it. Other guy looks over, you nod, he stops bidding. Sold! Two excavators—for fifty-five thousand dollars more than the figure you're getting for the entire five-piece deal. Plus another ten for the bribe! Sold! At a big loss! To the guy who showed up without doing his homework!"

"Who'd you say you were, again?" Krol's throat needed clearing.

"That answer in moments."

"Get there fast."

"The guy you bribed tells you where to meet in the parking lot, where the cameras don't cover, you do it, you pay him, he leaves. Situation situated! But before you can go back in, suddenly here's the auctioneer, and guess what. He wants to talk to you about the Sherman Act. Which I'm guessing you'd never heard of before you had your fifteen-year-old daughter violate it."

"I know the fucking Sherman Act."

"Oh, you do." The visitor put his hands up. "I didn't know. So the auctioneer says I can have you arrested, right now, you and your little… whatever. Or you can give me twenty thousand dollars, get your machines, and get out. Wow," he said brightly. "It's like I was right there, isn't it? How could I know so much about this?"

Krol's eyes were glinting.

"So then!" The visitor's face lit and he chuckled. "You argue with him! *I'm not giving you twenty grand!*" He shook his head again. "He even laughed when he told me about it. So he says, *You come in here, break a Federal law, don't cut me in, and now you think you're haggling? Okay, big shot.* Takes out his phone, dials, and you're like, *Okay, five,* and he says, *Yeah, let me talk to so and so*—and you go, *Ten,* and he says, *Tell him it's*—and you go, *Twenty!* and he says, *Oh, sorry, wrong number*, and hangs up. He didn't call the Feds, by the way. That was me he was talking to the whole time. So you pay him his twenty, and you go back in and start making new pickup arrangements, since you don't have enough cash now. But at least now you know a crooked auctioneer you can use some other time, right? Only you can't. You know why? Because you're never going back to Ohio again. Because Ohio's mine. That's who I am."

Krol didn't respond. The visitor stared at him. "The auction's mine. The auctioneer's mine. Half your twenty K was in my pocket that afternoon, and I had people looking at this Thomas Krol, who came into my territory half-assed with an underaged little girl."

Krol put his hand on the revolver on the little counter.

"Before you do," the visitor cautioned. "There is no chance you survive that. Think about my level of preparation. I don't walk in here until I have every single thing set up. Somebody's already in the right place to kill you if I don't walk out.

"Or," he said, after a pause, "if you follow me after I do.

"Or," he said, as the frozen silence continued, "we can get back to making your ex disappear."

"What do you care about that?" Krol's throat still needed clearing. His hand was still on the gun.

"Like I said up front. When you get what you want, I get what I want."

"What I hear you saying," Krol said slowly, "is if I shoot you, Ohio's mine."

"Because all my people will suddenly take orders from you?" The visitor didn't hide his amusement. "But, long as we're talking about my people. The one who's set up to kill you if I don't walk out of here healthy? Is eager to do it. You'll die. They'll enjoy it."

"But then all the things you said would happen to me will happen to them, right? They don't want to lose everything or go to prison either."

"They don't care. You do."

"Why don't they care."

The visitor considered. "Let's just leave it at loyalty. So, if you'll please take your hand off that firearm, I'll continue to explain." When Krol didn't move, he said mildly, "For god's sake, Tom. I'm locked in a hole, unarmed, and you're standing next to a gun. Come on."

Krol took his hand off the gun, but he didn't move away from it. "Talk," he said.

"Uh—" The visitor looked up, finding his place. "Right. My territory, half-assed. So. You didn't know who you were dealing with, did you. The other bidder and the auctioneer? Could have been honest and gone to law enforcement. Your little forger? Could have caused a scene. Three games of Russian roulette? You let the other people load the guns all three times. You got lucky. You got taken, sure. But you also got lucky, because you got me knocking on the door today instead of the FBI."

"Does the FBI talk less?"

The visitor smiled briefly. Then he considered the question.

"No," he said.

"You going to tell me what you want now?"

"Yeah. Though I wasn't positive until I got down here and got a good look at you."

"So?"

"Your operation's too small. I can't do business with you." He shook his head. "The numbers won't work out."

"I have a bigger operation than it looks like down here."

"Yeah. Not big enough. Maybe another few years. But not now. You're still selling hot excavators at a discount because one big client backed out."

Krol drew in a long breath and let it out. "Something's not making sense. You don't want to do business…."

"No."

"But you also haven't killed me."

"Right. The cost to benefit doesn't make sense. Just like you taking out your ex. The numbers don't work out. Everything comes down to numbers."

"Walk me through those numbers."

"I did. Cost of the hit itself, cost of— Oh, you don't mean the numbers to kill Ruby Charles. You mean the numbers to kill Tom Krol. Why would I tell Tom Krol the Tom Krol numbers?"

"I'm still confused. If I'm too small to do business with, but you also don't want to-—oh." Krol looked at him long, then nodded. "*Maybe another few years.* I get it. You noticed me because I got bigger, and you want to neutralize me before I'm big enough to threaten you." He began to nod. "You're here to keep me out of Ohio. Getting rid of Ruby's just a deal-sweetener."

The visitor was watching him. "You're a smart man."

"And all of that costs less than killing me. How much less?"

"Doesn't matter. Even a penny less swings the decision."

"If chasing me off costs one penny less than killing me, you don't kill me?"

"Sure. I mean, there are guesses, but once you reach your numbers, those are your numbers."

"One penny more and you do kill me."

"Sure."

Rocking slightly on the balls of his feet, Krol said, "Ten mil."

"Ten mil... what?"

"If taking out some middle-aged housewife out is gonna end up costing me one point four, taking me out has got to cost you at least ten. So that's my price for going away. No—sorry." He corrected himself. "One penny less, right? So nine hundred ninety-nine thousand, nine hundred ninety-nine, and ninety-nine cents. Pay up, save your penny, and I never set foot in Ohio again."

"Really."

"Really."

"All right. Two things. Number two is, there is no number two, and number one is, you don't get shit from me."

"Really. What happened to above the line, this, below the line, that? Maybe that was just bullshit?"

"I brought a bag of carrots." The visitor pantomimed lifting it. "I brought a bag of sticks. I brought no bag of bullshit."

Krol sniffed carefully. "Smells like it to me."

The visitor grinned. "Nah. Look. If I give you ten mil, now you've got seven more zeroes to use against me, but I've got seven fewer to use against you."

"Sounds like you're looking for a guarantee. I don't see how you get that unless you kill me."

"Can I finish explaining my plan? It's a good plan."

"Oh, sorry, yeah. My bad." Krol nodded over-solicitously. "Absolutely."

"Great. Carrot number one: Exactly what your ad said you wanted. She's gone." He snapped his fingers. "Like that. Yeah, I can do it. Carrot number two, you never become a suspect. Nobody ever investigates you for murder."

"Why not?"

"What's the absolute safest way to get rid of someone?"

"Talk them to death?"

"If that worked, I wouldn't need somebody waiting for you with a gun. Ways to get rid of someone." He counted on his fingers. "One, kill them. Problems there, already gone over. Two, scare them. Problems there, what if they don't scare? What if they stop being scared and get angry? If I scare Tom Krol, I just end up pissing off a smart guy with resources. If you scare Ruby Charles, you end up pissing off a smart woman who's already got restraining orders on you, plus her five brothers and one sister."

"She's not as smart as she thinks she is."

"Oh, a dumb research librarian. Okay."

"Neither are her brothers."

"Look, point being—" The visitor paused. "I'd be more worried about the sister. Look. Point being, scaring people always comes back on you. So—can't kill 'em, can't scare 'em. What is the safest way to make someone go away? Not just safe, but ironclad?" He paused again. Krol didn't answer. "Well, in my experience, the purest, most beautiful way? Is if they drop everything and wander away. By themselves."

"You think I'm going to wander away."

"One thing at a time. We're talking about how I'm going to make your ex disappear. All I have to do is give her what she truly wants from you, and then? She leaves you alone."

"You—that's…. What exactly do you think she truly wants from me?"

"What do *you* think she wants from you?"

Krol looked at him like he was stupid. "All my money?"

"And?"

"She's a psycho bitch."

"Educate me."

"What the fuck do you think she wants? My money. My head on a platter. My balls in a vise."

"And?"

"And nothing, what do you—she's psycho."

The visitor shook his head. "That's not it. That's not even close."

"Oh, really, you're an expert? "

"You're seeing her from your perspective. You're not seeing yourself from hers."

"Okay, expert, what's her *perspective*?"

"You know things about her that I can't. Memories from dating, marriage, children, divorce… a lot of it isn't even conscious. When I tell you what she wants, *those very things I can't know* are going to be what tell you I'm right. You'll know it instantly, in your bones, that I'm absolutely dead-on correct."

After a moment, Krol said, "Are you going to tell me, or—"

"She wants you out of her daughters' lives."

Krol closed his mouth.

"Permanently," the visitor said. "With certainty. Gone."

Krol started to shake his head, stopped. Started to talk, didn't.

"All those other things? Money? Balls in a vise? She doesn't really want those. She settles for them, because they're the most she thinks she can get."

Krol started to talk again, didn't again.

"She gets what she really wants?" the visitor said. "She's gone."

Krol's head was shaking. The visitor said, "You're seeing it even better than I can."

"Give her the girls," Krol said.

The visitor waited.

"Give her..."

"Smart people consider everything, Tom. But that's not actually what I'm saying. What I am saying is give her a piece of theater."

"Get the fuck out of here."

"All right." The visitor turned and went toward the exit. When he was a few steps up, Krol said, "What the fuck does that mean?"

"What?"

"A piece of theater."

"Am I answering that, or am I getting the fuck out?"

"Just tell me what it means."

"Okay." The visitor came back down the steps. "You're her. One day you text your ex."

"About what."

"Doesn't matter. You want something. His balls in a vise. All his hard-earned money. He doesn't answer. What do you do? You're her."

"Is this the theater?"

"What do you *do*, Tom?"

"Keep texting."

"No answer."

"Have the girls text him."

"Still no answer. Now what?"

"Email, text, call him, ride his ass..."

"No response. How long do you keep this going?"

"'Til he...." Krol gestured vaguely.

"There is no *'til he*. No responses, no read receipts. How long before you drive to his place?"

"Uh… Depends on how bad she wants some money. A week. Five days."

"Buzz the door—" The visitor pantomimed it. "Bzzt. No answer. What do you do?"

"Walk the fence, see if I can see in."

"Nothing. Now what?"

"You tell me."

"Tom. *You know her.* What does she *do*? We know what she does for a living. Does she break out those skills?"

"No…. Maybe a…. She comes out with the girls. They know the door code."

"The girls open the door for the mama. Who comes in? The whole troop?"

"No…. Just her."

"Right, in case there's a body. What do you do?"

"Uh. Go through his stuff."

"Doesn't tell you anything. Now what? Go home? Research obituaries, arrest records, hospitals, right? Still nothing. He's been gone a couple weeks, now. What are you thinking?"

"He went out of town."

"Went out? Or skipped out?"

"Nah." Krol shook his head. "You think she'll give up if she thinks I skipped, but she won't. She'll keep on looking."

"Because you still have the things she's willing to settle for— your money, your balls, all that. The stuff that's not what she really wants. As long as she thinks you're findable, she's gonna get what she's entitled to."

"Psycho. Bitch," Krol said.

"A woman tricked and cheated. A *research librarian* tricked and cheated. There's nothing to make her stop. Until when?"

Krol laughed. "Until when. Forever. The end of time."

"Okay. In the meantime, where has Tom been?"

"It's your story."

"*No*, Tom. It's your story. You know where you've been? Anywhere you want. Doing anything you want. Doing anyone you want. Off the grid."

"Sounds fun."

"Just not Ohio."

"Sure."

"Or one other place, that I'll get to. But you're not entirely at ease."

"That's sad. Why not?"

"You said it already. She won't stop. Now, here's where I need you to make a leap. We're no longer talking about anyone in particular. We're talking about generic people. Generic guy, generic ex-wife. Forget individual personalities. We're looking at a *principle*. All right?"

"Dazzle me."

"Is it sensible, *in principle*, that when you give generic people the one thing they truly want, they drop the things they never really wanted in the first place and go away?"

"I mean—sure. But you don't know—"

"I got that. I hear you. But we agree that it's sensible in general, so just—stay with me."

Krol's head shaking continued, doubtfully.

"One day her mail comes. And hey, look, an envelope from you! Postmarked... I don't care. Anywhere. Rio. Cancun. Doesn't matter. Tahoe."

"Great. What's in it?"

Now the visitor smiled. Spreading his arms, warmly, he said, *"Blue skies."*

Krol looked blank.

The visitor dropped his arms. "Remember what we said you're giving her."

"You said theater."

"Right." He took the envelope from his shirt pocket. Selecting a crisply folded paper from it, he said, "And here it is."

Krol took it. His eyes returned several times to the top of the page.

"Copied over in your own handwriting, obviously," the visitor said.

"What the fuck?"

"Which part isn't clear?"

"All of it!"

The visitor looked perplexed, took it back, and read from it. "You don't get my money anymore. The girls are all yours, permanently. Fuck you, fuck them, don't look for me, don't talk to the cops, tell the girls I had to leave and don't try to contact me or they'll get hurt. And then some more fuck-yous, and you know, like that." He looked up.

"Why would I send her this?"

"Oh—well, remember what she truly wants. Here it is. *The girls are yours, permanently.* And when that really sinks in? And Tom's still not answering? Now she believes you're not just gone for a while. You've skipped."

Krol stared at him.

"I see you get it." the visitor said. "You feel it. *She believes it.*"

After a pause, Krol said, "She won't believe it." Then, more firmly, "She won't believe it."

"Back up a few seconds, to your first reaction, when you felt it along with her—"

"It doesn't matter." Krol's head was shaking. "Sure, maybe she'll feel it for a minute, like I did. She'll think I've skipped—but then it'll go away, same as it did with me. She'll never believe I'm giving up my kids."

"That's your final answer?"

"Yeah. She won't."

"Good!" The visitor looked pleased. "Very good. And that brings us to the final part of the presentation. We're now at *Proof.* I'm going to prove to you that she will believe this letter. Think I can do it?"

Krol had his amused face back on. "Sure, whatever you say."

"I say—" With a flourish, the visitor produced another folded paper from the envelope. "That I can. Oh." The visitor tilted the paper slightly away as Krol began to reach. "You're not going to like everything in here. Please don't go for the gun again."

He handed it over.

"Voluntary termination..." Krol said, reading it.

"...of parental rights. See, first she reads T*he girls are all yours, permanently.* And she does feel it. Just like you did. But before she can stop believing, bam! Right behind it? This. *Voluntary Termination of Parental Rights.* And—still no responses from Tom. For some time now. Now does she truly believe you've skipped?"

"Tell me why I care about that, again?"

"Because that's when she vanishes from your life. I said I could make her disappear and no one would investigate you for it. Here you go. She's gone. Boom."

"And... I'm in Rio."

"Wherever. Thailand, Spain. Wherever you want."

"But... I'm not *staying* there, so...soon as I come back, we're right back where we started."

"Ah." The visitor raised a forefinger. "We're not at the end of the 'Proof' section yet."

He handed over the rest of the envelope. Krol slid the first paper out, unfolded it, read it, and looked up.

"Letter to the IRS," the visitor said.

"Letter to the state," he said, as Krol sorted through the rest. "Letter to local police. Letter to Ohio state police. Letter to ATF. Letter to the FBI. Letter to CPS. Letter to School Safety. Letter to school psychologist. Letter to DOJ, why the hell not. All about you. All seeded with information that will turn out to be one hundred percent accurate."

Krol's stillness came back.

The visitor said, "All those *ifs* you pointed out? *If* the IRS notices you? *If* you light up the state system? *If* the cops pull that zipper? Now they're not ifs."

There was no clear response from Krol. His head moved a little, his mouth opened a little and just hung that way.

"We're done with the carrots." The visitor lifted the second imaginary bag. "Now we're into the sticks."

"You *are* here to blackmail me."

"No, no. Blackmail is the threat of doing something bad. This isn't a threat. It's already done. Look at the dates on those letters. Already mailed. Oh!" From his back pocket, he pulled another paper, folded roughly to fit in the pocket. "Sorry about the creases. I've been sitting on it since it came out of your mailbox. Letter *from* the IRS, confirming your appointment here, at nine a.m. tomorrow morning."

"Why would you—what did—"

"That's why I'm here today. They're coming tomorrow. I left you time to run."

"This isn't real." Looking at the creased letter. "How do I know this is real?"

"Call them. Plus, think about—" He cut himself off. "Go for that gun and you won't live."

They were both extremely still.

"You're awfully sure of yourself," Krol said.

"I'm not who I'm awfully sure of."

"What if I just shoot you and take my chances?"

"Then we both die. But Tom." The visitor leaned in. "This is your blue sky, too. Not just hers. This is what every prepper dreams of, right? The shit really does hit the fan, and you finally grab that go bag and go. And at the same time, it's what every man with a psycho ex-wife dreams of, too. Because where you go? Is somewhere beautiful. No kids to pay for. No ex to break your balls. Just you and the white sands. Or the red neon, or whatever your heart truly desires. The new empire. The blue skies. The women. It's true I'm the one giving you the nudge." He nodded. "But I don't think I have to push too hard. Grab that gold ring—and go."

"Go anywhere."

"Just not Ohio, and not here. Set foot either place, things go bad. Other than that, yeah. Absolutely anywhere."

"Things go bad how."

"Use your imagination."

Krol's hand moved to hover near the revolver.

"You know what happens if you do," the visitor said. "Now, here's how I'll know you accepted my terms, because it's a lot to take in, and I don't expect the answer today. There are eyes on Ruby's mail. When you mail that letter and the Voluntary Termination form, you're not just sending her a message—you're sending me one: *I accept your terms, and I'm gone.*"

"And if I don't accept your terms?"

"You'll need an army you don't have."

"And when do I come back?"

"Come back?" The visitor looked surprised. "I suppose when you want to be arrested. Or dead. Depending on who gets to you first." He stopped and thought. He nodded. "Dead."

Krol swept the revolver up to aim it at the visitor's head. His lips were parted.

"Okay," the visitor said, glancing at it. "I'm out of here. Don't answer her or your kids any more. Radio silence began when I walked in here." He looked briefly at the picture again before turning and starting for the steps. Partway up, he said, "Unlock the door or shoot me, Tom."

* * * *

A black screen curtain hung in the house's side door. The visitor had a white envelope in his breast pocket. This time it was a blue Polo shirt. He was carrying a brown paper bag. He went up the wooden porch steps.

In the kitchen, brownie makings and crumbs were scattered over the counter. A curling photo, held on the refrigerator by magnet poetry, was the same one he'd seen on Krol's wall, only the woman wasn't cropped out. All three smiled at the camera. In another photo at a lake, all three were older.

The kitchen window overlooked a half-wild backyard with vegetables in a small patch and a much-weathered treehouse in the clutches of an old birch. A shower was running upstairs. He set the bag on the kitchen table and went toward the sound, stepping where the stairs didn't squeak. No one was in the three lightly cluttered bedrooms at the top. A small table on the landing held a fish tank with no water in it and an air pump still in its package. Tinny music played in the bathroom.

The bathroom door made no sound as he pushed it open. The music was coming from a phone on a shelf. The shower was blasting. He set the envelope on the toilet seat.

Downstairs, he sat at the table and waited.

The rasp of the pipes stopped. Soon feet thumped down the staircase and there were authoritative little rips as the envelope was opened. The feet stopped short of the kitchen doorway. Paper slid and unfolded.

The person beyond the doorway inhaled sharply. The paper flapped. "What—" said a woman's stunned voice.

As the visitor waited, the woman stepped into the kitchen, still reading. She had damp hair. A towel was wrapped around her. The visitor watched her. Her jaw was dropped.

The hand holding the papers went to her chest and she saw him.

After their gazes locked, she made a calming gesture with her other hand and brought the papers away from her chest to look at them again. "I'm sorry," she said distantly. She went back to the top of the first page and scanned it more closely. Then she looked at the Voluntary Termination form, and her jaw dropped again, but not as far.

She glanced at him. "Did you dye your hair?"

"I dyed it back."

"I support you in whatever you do." She was back to reading. She stopped to look at him again. "Are you back for good?"

"I just needed some time."

"I'm glad to see you."

"I'm glad to see you too," he said and took pastries and coffee out of the bag as she went back to reading.

*   *   *   *

He made a phone call, sitting on her back porch in the dimming light, watching kids run in and out of the thicket at the back of the yard.

When Ruby's sister answered, he said, "You can put away that shotgun."

"He sent the letter?"

"She's at the police station with it now."

"Is she scared?"

"She's in take-charge mode."

"Did she tell the girls? How are the girls?"

"Not yet. They're…" He watched them vanish into the trees. "They're having a good time right now."

There was a long silence. "If that piece of shit comes back, I will happily go to prison."

"I know," he said. "So does he. He just doesn't know it'll be you."

"Does she suspect anything?"

"She noticed I dyed my hair."

"I thought you dyed it back."

"That's what she noticed."

"Oh."

"I'm going to let her chalk it up to my time off from the relation-ship."

"You did look pretty different with the hair. And the nose. If he ever does come back, I don't think he'll recognize you. If he does, I'll get him quick as I can."

"I appreciate that, thank you." He paused. "I kept the nose."

"I thought we said—"

"We did. I just—want it. It's not like it'll mean anything to any-one."

"It's a loose end."

"It's a latex nose. I'll buy some funny glasses and a mustache and stick them all in the same shoebox."

She was silent. "Think of it as his scalp," he said. "You can come over and fondle it once in a while."

She made a disapproving noise.

Jody burst out of the thicket, shrieking, and he was on his feet be-fore he knew it, no longer aware of the phone at his ear. She reached the birch tree and shot up its nailed footholds into the treehouse. Two more girls tore out of the trees, also shrieking, and followed her beck-oning. The treehouse creaked and thudded as they landed in it. Irene emerged from the trees, stomping officiously, brandishing something. Possibly a dead bird.

Ruby's sister said, "Hello?"

"Sorry," he said after a couple more hellos. "Just the kids." He sat back down.

"Tell her I'm bringing potato salad on Saturday and I love her."

"I will."

She didn't hang up. "I wish to god I could have been the one down there."

This was a repeated conversation. He said his line. "He wouldn't have taken you seriously."

"I know. It had to be someone he didn't know. A *man* he didn't know. I know. I just wish."

"And then you'd have shot him."

"Abusive, sexist, piece-of-shit motherfucker."

"Look at the bright side. If he does come back, he can learn something new about women, and you can go to prison. Win-win."

She snorted. Then she said, "Thank you."

"It was my privilege."

"So, when you putting a ring on—"

"See you Saturday," he said, and hung up.

The sky was mostly dark now. "Blue skies," he said, and went to tell the girls to wash up.

✗

Keith Snyder lives in Connecticut with two teenagers and six bicycles.

A UNICORN IN THE HAREM

ELIZABETH ZELVIN

"Excellency," the prostrate eunuch said, "I wish to apprentice to the physician Reuven Hekim."

The Kizlar Agha stroked the white egret feather tucked into a fold of his turban and secured by a ruby, his forefinger caressing the soft curve at its tip.

"Reuven the Jew?"

"He is highly regarded in the Sublime One's household, where on occasion he attends the Sultan himself."

The boy's head bobbed on the slender stalk of his neck as he tried to discern the Kizlar Agha's reaction to his petition while maintaining a suitably humble posture.

"Oh, get up, boy," the Kizlar Agha said irritably. "You will get a spasm of the neck and require a physician yourself. What makes you think that Reuven Hekim will be willing to teach you?"

"He already has one apprentice," the eunuch said, "a young Jew named Ezra. Surely it will be no more trouble to tutor two than one."

"What do I care what his name is?" the Kizlar Agha snapped. Five years ago, he would have known this eunuch's name. The eunuchs of the harem were his children, his responsibility, his eyes and ears. He could still tell a Nubian from an Abyssinian, but he was beginning to think of the new ones as Prettyboy 17, Prettyboy 18, and so on. That would never do. He scowled. "If you have approached the *hekim* without asking my permission first, I am seriously displeased."

"Of course not, Excellency!" the boy cried. "It was Ezra who thought such an argument would persuade his master. He is a most intelligent and respectable Jew, the son of Diego Mendoza, a merchant who is well regarded throughout Istanbul."

Ha! The Kizlar Agha's eyes gleamed. He knew Mendoza's sister very well indeed. But the boy—Enis, that was it—need not know that. So a nephew of Kira Rachel, purveyor to Sultan Suleiman's harem, studied with the Sultan's most favored Jewish physician and had befriended one of the Kizlar Agha's own charming eyes-and-ears. Life was about to get interesting. It happened all too seldom.

"A eunuch physician would be fit to attend the ladies," he said, "and thus of use to the *haremlik*. I will speak to Reuven Hekim myself."

* * * *

"Do you believe, Kira Rachel," the Kizlar Agha asked, "that unicorn horn cures plague and helps men sire children?"

The two sat sipping mint tea from glasses in filigree holders.

"Do you believe," Rachel asked, "that there is such an animal as a unicorn?"

"If there is not," he said, "how do you account for the fact that so many people swear that they have seen one?"

"I suspect, *effendi*," Rachel said, "that these people have heard of someone who once spoke to someone who once met someone who swore that he had seen some kind of animal, glimpsed for a moment, that might have had a horn on its forehead or perhaps on its nose."

"You may be right," the Kizlar Agha said. "I myself, as a youth in Africa, more than once saw an animal with a horn on its nose. It was squat and ugly, not resembling a fleet and delicate horse in any particular. But some kind of horn is called a unicorn's and valued as a remedy."

"Many people swear that Jews have horns," Rachel said. "I *know* that to be false. But their conviction cannot be shaken. People believe what they want to believe."

"And the horn's power to bestow potency?"

"According to my nephew, his teacher Reuven Hekim says, 'such remedies have no efficacy save by the occasional coincidence that fans the flames of folly in the credulous.'"

"A nice turn of phrase, but not one I can repeat to the Grand Vizier." The Kizlar Agha shifted from one broad buttock to the other on his swans-down cushions. "You will divulge what I tell you now to no one."

"Certainly not, *effendi*."

"You know the Grand Vizier, Ibrahim Pasha, is to marry Princess Hadije in two weeks."

"With great pomp and ceremony," she said. "You cannot mean that *he* needs unicorn horn for such a purpose."

"The gentleman walks a narrow bridge above a raging flood. All his powers flow from the Sultan, who raised him from a tribute boy, a Christian captive, converted and educated him, and bestowed wealth and high office upon him. Now he embraces him as family, giving Ibrahim his sister in marriage. He makes him a *damad*, the Valide's son-in-law, since his own daughter is still an infant. No woman in the Empire has more power than the Sultan's mother. He has even sworn Ibrahim an oath that whatever happens, he will never execute him."

"A rare concession indeed," Rachel murmured. *Ottomans!*

"With so much depending on this marriage," the Kizlar Agha said, "Ibrahim Pasha knows he must keep Princess Hadije happy."

"Especially on the wedding night," Rachel said.

"I am assured assistance is not *necessary*," he said, silently thanking Allah for sending him the company of a quick-witted woman who was trying neither to kill him nor to topple him from power. "But it would relieve anxiety. Since he can confide in no one without risking intrigue or scandal, he came to me."

"But, *effendi*—"

"I am no one when I need to be." He smiled a crocodile smile. "I told him I could supply a go-between of the utmost discretion. Reuven Hekim will be told only that unicorn horn is required. You will arrange the rest. I do not wish to know the details."

* * * *

Reuven ben Pinchas of Zamora, who had studied medicine in Salamanca and been expelled from Spain in 1492, had not expected to spend his later years in the great Palace of Suleiman the Magnificent. He was treated well and not unhappy. Unlike the Spanish Christians, these Turks would even listen courteously when one explained that the surest guard against infection was cleanliness.

"You are reading Torah to the rabbi, *hekim*," his apprentice, young Ezra, said when he embarked on his favorite lecture. "I will not forget to cleanse my hands every time I touch a bleeding or infected patient."

"We must teach not only our patients but every soul we encounter to do the same." Reuven's shaggy brows twitched, and his bushy beard, always in need of a clipping, bobbed as he chewed on his lower lip. "The Palace is kept reasonably clean. But the poor of Istanbul may chase the rats from their dwellings now and then, even cleanse with fire after a plague scare, but that is all. Working folk may launder their clothes but not bathe their bodies. Against illness, they demand talismans, swearing they are more efficacious than our simple herbal remedies."

"The ladies of the harem cherish their talismans, too," Enis said. "If they ask for a remedy, it is never stinging nettle or oregano tea but some nostrum such as dragon's blood from Cathay or the horn of a unicorn. What use can they possibly have for that?"

"What, indeed?" The newcomer entered the room in a swirl of blue robes and threw back her hood with a practiced motion.

"Aunt Rachel!"

"Kira Rachel, your fame precedes you," Hekim Reuven said, advancing with a broad smile. "You are welcome here."

She shook off her veil, revealing a merry face with laugh lines crinkling the outer corners of her bright brown eyes.

"I am honored to make your acquaintance, Reuven Hekim. I could not help hearing. Do you *have* unicorn horn?"

"The Sultan insists that I have every remedy in the known world on hand," the physician said. "Is this a social call, or is there some way in which I can serve you?"

Rachel admitted she had sought out the physician on a private matter. Once she had assured Ezra that she was in perfect health, as were his uncle Ümīt and the children, Reuven shooed the boys out, and she was able to reveal her errand.

"Since unicorn horn has been mentioned," she said, "wait until tomorrow. Then make up a package. Tell Enis to bring it to the *haremlik* and slip it inside my trunk when no one is looking, including me. And thank you for asking no questions."

"I am at your service," he said.

The great trunk always remained open for much of the afternoon, so the ladies could peruse her wares. With the royal wedding plans at fever pitch, there was plenty to provide distraction. At the end of the day, she would simply close the trunk and take it home.

She thanked the doctor, invited him to Shabbat dinner the following week, and left his sanctum, happy to have discharged her duty and made a friend.

* * * *

Four days before the royal wedding, when Rachel arrived in the *haremlik*, the *hatuns* swarmed around her, buzzing not with demands to see the latest baubles in her trunk and hear the news of the outside world, but about an exciting event of their own.

"The artificer from Cathay has come," Dilara Hatun said, "with fireworks for the Princess's wedding! The main displays will take place during the festivities, where the Court and the populace can see them. But the Sublime One has decreed a special display for our pleasure. The artificer will have a chance to test his newest effects— for a royal wedding, the display must be unique. We will sit behind a wooden lattice with a sheer veil to look through."

"How splendid," Rachel said. "When does this festive event take place?"

"This afternoon!" young Elmas Hatun said, dancing with excitement. "Everything must be perfect for the wedding itself. But *we* get to see the fireworks first!"

"Do not bounce, Elmas," Aysun Hatun said with a sniff. "It is unseemly. I am not surprised that *your* idea of pleasure is a box of sticky sweetmeats and an explosion in the sky."

"You have been grumpy ever since Hürrem caught the Sultan's eye," Elmas said.

"Do not bully her," Halime Hatun said. "We are all looking forward to this diversion, and no one wants a black cloud hanging over it."

What an excellent distraction, Rachel thought.

Where was Enis? Had he hidden the unicorn horn in the trunk yet? She looked around the vast chamber with its thick carpets, flickering filigreed lamps, rich, heavy drapes, and alcoves barely screened by sheer embroidered curtains. She could not see him. On the nearest occupied couch, someone with rich auburn hair was having her toenails buffed and painted.

Hürrem, the *haseki*—the Sultan's Favorite, no one else in the harem had such hair—turned her head.

"Kira Rachel," she said. "You will have trouble keeping their attention on your wares today. The silly peahens think it was my Sultan's idea to give them such a treat."

Hürrem smiled the mysterious half smile that was fast becoming as much her signature as the broad grin that had caused Suleiman to name her the Merry One. She probably practiced that smile in the excellent mirror of coated glass which Rachel had sent for from Venice and sold her at a tidy profit. Had she really proposed the fireworks for the *hatuns*? It might as easily have been the Valide or the princess. To smile and say nothing was a good trick. Rachel used it in business negotiations all the time.

"Would you like to look through my trunk yourself, *hatun*?" she asked.

"My Sultan gives me everything I need," the *haseki* said.

"Do you attend the fireworks?" Rachel asked.

"I will attend the wedding festivities along with the Valide and the princesses," Hürrem said. "A temporary *haremlik* is being constructed, and the highest ladies will attend the bride on henna night and in the *hammam*."

A frown rippled across her brow and vanished.

She wishes she hadn't said so much, Rachel thought. She regrets boasting about her consequence.

"Of course, *hatun*," she said. "I understand."

"Don't humor me, *kira*," Hürrem said, the grin that had enchanted the Sultan breaking out like sunlight on her face. "We are both too intelligent not to be honest once in a while. If you do not cross me, we can be allies."

Once Hürrem's beautification ritual was complete, she disappeared in the direction of her own sumptuous apartments. Rachel did not want to hover near her trunk, but she couldn't help looking back toward it now and then. She had not seen Enis approach it by the time chosen for the fireworks display. There was a great hubbub as the chattering women hurried toward the appointed courtyard and settled onto the cushions piled high for their comfort behind the veiled wooden lattice. Rachel, torn between watching the display herself and keeping an eye on the trunk, was startled to hear muffled sobbing coming from a curtained alcove.

"Hello?" she said softly. "Who is it? Can I help?"

The sobbing faded to a stifled whimper.

"It's Kira Rachel," she said. "May I come in? I won't tell anyone. Maybe I can help."

"No one can help. *Please* go away."

Rachel pushed aside the curtain just enough to slip inside the alcove. The interior was so dim that she could barely see its occupant, a slight young thing crouched beneath a pile of cushions. Shielding her face with her arm, she curled herself up into a tight ball. Rachel knelt beside her.

"You are new, are you not? What is your name, my dear?"

"Nermin," the girl whispered. "It means 'delicate.' They told me to forget my old name."

"Sometimes," Rachel said, "it is easier to adjust to a completely new and different life if you embrace it completely, leaving the past behind, however hard that may be."

"Have you ever had to do that?" the girl asked, lifting her wet face to Rachel's.

"More than once," Rachel said, "and every time my life depended on it."

"But you are strong," Nermin said. "I want to go home!"

She broke down again. This time she sobbed silently, and Rachel took her in her arms and rocked her, as she would have had the girl been one of her own daughters.

Eventually Nermin could cry no more. Then Rachel had to assure her several times that apologies were unnecessary and advise her how best to disguise the reddened eyes and swollen nose that would betray that she had been weeping.

Rachel had just offered to bring her a vial of rosewater to bathe her eyes and a soothing lotion containing honey, jasmine, and healing herbs when a commotion broke out at the far end of the *haremlik*. While they talked, Rachel had been aware of a series of booms that she took to be the promised fireworks. Now screams and cries ensued, along with billowing puffs of smoke and an influx of terrified *hatuns* colliding, as they scurried back to the safety of the harem, with a more organized chain of eunuchs with buckets throwing water on charred wood—all that remained of the temporary latticework—scorched cushions, and whatever items the ladies had left behind in their haste to flee the fire.

Rachel rushed to slam down the lid of her trunk. She hoped that the smell of smoke had not affected any of her velvet brocades or silks and that Enis had had a chance to slip the unicorn horn inside the trunk while she was with Nermin, if not earlier. No one would be buying cloth or jewelry or books today. The *hatuns* found her portable bazaar exciting only because, usually, nothing more exciting happened here. She hoped Nermin had enough wit to slip away while everyone's attention was elsewhere. Rachel's priority was to get her trunk out of the Palace and home.

* * * *

"Missing!" the Kizlar Agha thundered. Few eunuchs could thunder, but the Kizlar Agha was a big man who had held authority under four Sultans and had had plenty of practice. "No concubine of Suleiman, Sultan of Sultans, Khan of Khans, Commander of the Faithful, and Sovereign of the Three Cities goes missing! No lady in my charge goes missing! If she is not in the *haremlik*, she must be in the Palace, and if she is in the Palace, she must and will be found. Have every corner searched. Surely among the Sultan's slaves are some who know every corner—if not his eunuchs or his janissaries, his *cleaners* must know every corner. The Sublime One's *monkeys* must know every corner. So do not tell me she cannot be found! Come back only when you can tell me you have found her."

The Kizlar Agha had not allowed himself such a magnificent fit of rage in years. He was almost enjoying himself. But it was no laughing matter. Even the least of the *hatuns* was the Sultan's personal property. This little wisp of a thing, Nermin, that was it, new and likely to remain untouched, if Hürrem had her way, was not important in herself. But it would be best for all concerned if she were found hiding in the *haremlik* in a laundry basket or a giant oil jar like one of Ali Baba's thieves. Second best, however hardhearted of him to wish it, would be to find that she had drowned herself in one of the ornamental pools. The worst case would be if she had actually gotten *out*. In that case, she would still need to be found.

The eunuch who served as his eyes and ears at the Gate of Salutation approached.

"Kira Rachel wishes an audience, Excellency."

Rachel followed on the messenger's heels.

"I am missing a girl, *kira*," he said heavily, no longer stimulated by rage. Kira Rachel had a way of reminding him of his humanity. "Have you found one?"

"Alas, *effendi*, I am missing a certain item. It should have been in my trunk when I left the Palace. But when I reached home, it was not."

The Kizlar Agha waved his attendants out of earshot.

"When was it put in the trunk?" he asked.

"Sometime during the afternoon when the whole harem was watching the fireworks display."

"That is when my *hatun* went missing!" he exclaimed. "Was it in the trunk before the fire that disrupted the display?"

"I cannot tell you."

"Who can, then? Come, do not hesitate. We must explore all avenues."

"The eunuch Enis. He was entrusted to take it from the *hekim*'s sanctum to the *haremlik* and hide it in the trunk. I would swear that he is reliable."

"He must be questioned. Perhaps the girl Nermin spied on him and seized the opportunity to snatch up something valuable and flee."

"Nermin? Poor child!"

"You cannot champion them all, my *kira*. This one has not been here long. Do you know her well?"

"No-o-o," Rachel said. "I spoke with her yesterday. She was longing for her home."

"We have seen it before," he said, "the fantasy of wealth and flight. You know it leads only to death. The Sultan will not be thwarted. Come, turn your excellent brain to solving this mystery of the missing unicorn horn. Many eyes are searching for the girl. But I cannot afford to make an enemy of the Grand Vizier, who is also the Sultan's closest friend and will be the Valide's *damad*."

"Could the fire in the courtyard have been set on purpose?" Rachel asked. "It certainly caused maximum confusion—screaming, people running in all directions, and a great deal of smoke."

"I suppose the Cathayans might have been bribed to start the fire," the Kizlar Agha said. "I directed that only the eunuchs among his staff have contact with the harem. We must question them through the artificer, as the eunuchs speak only the tongue of Cathay."

"Please do not start torturing eunuchs just yet, *effendi*," she said. "It is exceedingly hard to bribe someone with whom you have no common language. Besides, their reputation was at stake. It would not have been worth the risk."

"We had better have young Enis in," the Kizlar Agha said.

"Do not alarm him, *effendi*," Rachel said. "Most folk tend to lie when they are frightened."

Enis was duly summoned. He knelt before the Kizlar Agha, looking apprehensive.

"Let me, *effendi*," Rachel said. "Enis, did you bring a sealed package into the *haremlik* yesterday afternoon at Reuven Hekim's request?"

"Yes, *kira*, I did."

"Do you know what it was?"

"No, *kira*. The *hekim* did not say, so I assumed he did not wish me to know."

"Were you not curious?" the Kizlar Agha asked.

"It is not my place to be curious, Excellency," Enis said.

"What did you do with it, Enis?" Rachel asked.

"I hid it in your trunk, as Reuven Hekim directed me to do. I tucked it into a fold of cloth near the bottom of a pile of heavy silk velvet brocades."

"Did you touch the lid?"

"No, I left it thrown back exactly as I found it."

"When did you do this?" Rachel asked. "I did not see you that afternoon at all."

"I saw you at the far end of the harem," Enis said, "talking to some of the *hatuns*. No one was near the trunk, so that is when I hid the package."

"Before the fireworks, then," she said.

"I saw Hürrem Hatun being groomed as well," he said. "I slipped away as you came toward her."

"I do not think he stole it," Rachel said after Enis had been dismissed. "When I visited Reuven Hekim, he was discussing unicorns and the horn's properties with his apprentices. I heard Enis say that the *hatuns* talked about it, but that he could not imagine what use they might have for it. Such naiveté is surely a mark of innocence."

"It does not take sophistication," the Kizlar Agha said, "to realize that a portable object of great value will always find a buyer in the Bedestan who will pay handsomely in gold for it."

"What use would Enis have for gold?" Rachel said. "You meet all his material needs, and his dream is to become a physician. When he is fully trained, he will be chief *hekim* to the harem."

"That does not put him in the clear," the Kizlar Agha said. "He might easily have guessed what the package contained."

"Reuven Hekim and I spoke privately," she said, "after turning the conversation to indifferent matters."

"Nonetheless," he said, "the boy knows more about the remedy than anyone else except ourselves and Reuven Hekim."

"Give me three days," Rachel said. "If I can find the stolen remedy and the girl, will you let me name my fee?"

"I do not think you mean to ask for gold," the Kizlar Agha said. "That would be too simple."

"Do not count the cost," she said, "until I have solved the puzzle."

* * * *

"Who are you?" Ezra demanded.

The skinny child crouching beneath the giant rosemary bush shrank back, setting its spicy leaves trembling with a faint fragrance.

"Don't be afraid," he said. "Are you waiting for Aunt Rachel? Come out of there. You'll get a cramp. It's all right. I'm a physician."

He held out his hand and waited patiently until she stood. She was slender but almost as tall as he—a young woman, not a child. Wide, dark eyes held his above her veil.

"You know Kira Rachel? She came, but she did not stay."

"She is my aunt. Perhaps I can help."

The skin was pale and fine around her eyes, the lashes dark and curling, the thin brows well tended. She was nothing like the robust market girls who worked the trunks at the Bedestan. Those girls sometimes twitched their veils aside and flashed their bare faces to tease a young man who was obviously not a Muslim. She seemed even more refined than Papa's business partner Amir's daughters. Amir had two wives. His womenfolk lived in a little *haremlik* in his home, but Ezra and his cousin Moshe had been sneaking peeks at them their whole lives.

"You cannot help. I must see Kira Rachel!"

"Then we had better go find her. She is probably next door, at my parents' house. Come."

Five minutes later, the girl was a puddle of sobs at Aunt Rachel's feet, and Aunt Rachel was shooing everyone out of the kitchen, including Mother.

"I am sorry to oust you from your own hearth, Joanna, but the girl needs warmth and privacy. See how she is shuddering."

"It is shock, Aunt Rachel," Ezra said. "You are right that heat is good for her. I can stay and—"

"Come along, dearest," Mother said. "Rachel knows what she is doing."

"My poor Nermin," Rachel was saying as they left. "How did you get out? Did you hide in my trunk?"

"No, *kira*. I did not wish you to be blamed if I were caught. I made my way through the Gates in the crowd and followed your cart all the way here."

"Let me see your feet. Oh, dear. Ezra must see to these blisters. He is a *hekim* and is sworn never to speak of a patient. Then you did not see anyone approach my trunk?"

"I don't understand, *kira*," Nermin said.

"In the *haremlik* or on the road," Rachel said, "did you see anyone hide something in the trunk or remove anything from it?"

"No, nothing."

"Did you hear any talk of unicorn horn among the women? Recently or at any time?"

"Some of the *hatuns* would mention it and laugh," Nermin said, "but I never understood the jokes."

"Are you sure you never saw such a thing?" Rachel asked. "You never possessed unicorn horn yourself or took it from the Palace? Speak truthfully, my dear."

"No, I swear it, *kira*," Nermin said. "A unicorn is big, is it not, like to a horse? How could I hide such a thing as its horn about my person, even if I had a use for it?"

* * * *

"I do not think the missing girl took it, *effendi*," Kira Rachel said.

"Why not?" the Kizlar Agha asked, taking a sip of sugary sherbet redolent of roses, sandalwood, and lemon. "For I know you do not merely *think*. You always have a reason."

"I cannot tell you yet," she said. "I have not yet completed my investigation."

"Hmmph. Have I no part to play?"

"Tell me about Ibrahim Pasha's enemies," she said. "Perhaps the thief is not someone who desires the horn but one who wishes to see the Grand Vizier discomfited. His plan to dazzle the princess with his enhanced virility is a great secret, but this palace is filled with holes."

"It is indeed hard to keep a secret," the Kizlar Agha said, "in this place, more city than dwelling, of airy walls and doors made of veils. Ibrahim Pasha has many enemies. They include all who wished to be appointed Grand Vizier, all who wished to become a royal *damad*, and all who envy his unprecedented personal intimacy with the Sultan—not to mention his vast wealth, his political power, and his military authority over the whole Army, excepting only the Sultan's janissaries. He is a charming man—he has thoroughly charmed the Sultan—but there are many men who think he grows too proud."

"Is there one who embodies all this envy in one person?" Rachel asked. "One, perhaps, who in the past had a close relationship with Ibrahim Pasha as well and might believe himself equally worthy of Ibrahim's luck? For he would surely see it as luck and not a reward for merits greater than his own. That is how the envious think."

"You are wise, my *kira*," he said. "I see envy in the harem as well. The least intelligent of my *hatuns*, who thinks Hürrem won Suleiman by her beauty, an accident of birth, and luck in his blindness to her own greater beauty, will never comprehend that Hürrem's chief advantages are her wit, intelligence, and sincere interest in the affairs of men and empires. Now let us speak of a man who fits the portrait you have painted to perfection. Yusef Pasha and Ibrahim entered the Enderun School together as boys of the *devşirme*. They were rivals in any study they undertook, but Ibrahim always had the edge. When Suleiman became Sultan, he recognized their talents, but only Ibrahim can call him friend. They rose in rank—Yusef is a general and a vizier—but only Ibrahim was appointed Beylerbeyi of Rumelia, that is, high lord of all the Ottoman lands in Europe."

"Would Yusef risk his career simply to embarrass Ibrahim?" Rachel asked.

"Ibrahim is not the Sultan," the Kizlar Agha said. "There is a faction that thinks he forgets that distinction and would enjoy seeing him taken down a peg. Ibrahim has unshakable confidence and pride. If that faith in himself could be shaken on his wedding night, many would be privately pleased."

"But you yourself said that he needs no assistance," Rachel said, "so why should his wedding night go badly for lack of the unicorn horn?"

"Ah, Kira Rachel, is it not you who say, 'People believe what they want to believe'?"

* * * *

"Rachel, I hope you are not planning to keep that girl," Joanna said, deftly braiding the long, thick strands of challah dough together and tucking and smoothing the ends. "Ezra is mooning over her like a lovesick puppy, and it will not do."

"What, do you have a nice Jewish girl lined up for him?" Rachel took a pinch of pistachios, dates, apricots, and honey she was preparing to spread on a broad, thin sheet of unbaked pastry from the mixing bowl and popped the mixture in her mouth. "And her name is Nermin. You *know* how it feels to be far from home, alone, and without power over your own life."

"I want my children to marry for love, as we did," Joanna said. "Yes, I have been powerless, without a soul to care what became of me, and sick with longing for a home that no longer exists. But she is not safe here, and neither are we while we harbor her."

"Her real name is Luljeta," Rachel said. "Pretty, isn't it? They told her to forget it when she entered the harem. She is from Albania, and far from encouraging unsuitable young love, I want to get her home."

"I suppose you want Diego to take her in one of his ships. Fan those coals, will you? I want to get this challah up to bake. Rachel! You'll set your hair on fire!"

Rachel knelt close to the hearth, her springy brown hair with its occasional glint of silver falling forward, just short of crisping range, as she flapped her kerchief vigorously at the glowing coals.

"I hope he won't have to. Luljeta has told me her story. Her twin brother was taken from their village by the *devşirme*. She thought he would be killed or enslaved and worked to death. Eventually some-one told her about the Enderun, how the boys convert and get an education that fits them to become janissaries, maybe generals or ad-mirals, and viziers or governors of provinces if they shine. She didn't know what to believe, so she set out to find him and see for herself."

"I can guess what happened next," Joanna said.

"Yes, she was captured by slavers. They sold her to a bey who thought she'd be of higher value to him as a gift to the Sultan, one beautiful virgin for an unspecified degree of royal gratitude, than as a toy to play with and pass on."

"And was the Sultan grateful?"

"Beautiful virgins are wasted on Suleiman," Rachel said. "He has eyes for no one but Hürrem. We must get Luljeta back to Albania as soon as possible. While she was in the harem, she managed to learn that her brother is a captain in the Ottoman Navy. His ship has been on an extended mission, but he must return to Istanbul soon, for there will be no campaigns while the heads of the military, the Sultan and Ibrahim, are celebrating the royal wedding. We will ask Amir to find him and explain the situation. Then it will be his job to get her home."

"Everyone knows that those raised in the Enderun are fanatically loyal to the Sultan," Joanna said. "He may deem it his duty to return her to the harem."

"She is his *twin sister*," Rachel said. "If he has any such notion, we will dissuade him."

* * * *

Ezra had never before ventured into these mean streets on the fringes of the Bedestan. There was a new moon, which meant no moon at all, just a few faint stars and flares from lamps stinking of cheap oil and fires that smelled as if the wood that fueled them had been eked out with camel dung. He wished that Enis were with him, but his fellow apprentice was confined to the Palace until the missing unicorn horn was found. That was why he was skulking from shabby hovel to tent to lean-to in the dark, following the Abyssinian eunuch Negasi, who was following a man too richly dressed for this neighborhood. He must be bent on some kind of mischief, or why would he be here, and why would Negasi, who was one of the Kizlar Agha's trusted servants, be following him?

Enis had been with him when the little procession set out, or Ezra would not have known Negasi's name. They had hoped Enis could slip through the outer gate undetected, but the Kizlar Agha's eyes-and-ears were sharp, and one of the gate-guard Nubians, tall as a tree, had stopped them, grinning at Enis without animus.

"Where do you think you're going, little brother? You know better. Our master says you must not pass the gate, and his word is law."

Enis had shrugged and turned back as if it were just a game, not a threat to his life if he could not prove he had not taken the horn and disposed of it. Let no one say a eunuch could not have courage!

"Go on, Ezra! Be vigilant. Do not lose them!"

Now the richly dressed man had stopped at a tent with faded red stripes and a red-shaded lantern over the entrance. He grasped the flap and paused for a moment. The light caught his upturned face. Ezra caught back a gasp, clasping his hands over his mouth to prevent any further sound from escaping. He recognized this man. He was someone important, a member of the Council and an enthusiastic follower of *cereed*, a team sport played with javelins on horseback and one at which Uncle Ümīt excelled. The janissaries had taught him long ago, when he and Papa and Aunt Rachel first came to Istanbul. The family sometimes joked that the real reason Uncle Ümīt had converted to Islam was so that he could join a top *cereed* team.

The man had entered the tent, but Ezra could hear his voice, loud and commanding. Now, what was his name? Yusef, that was it. He was a vizier. Where was Negasi? He had to peer through the shadows to locate him, crouched motionless with his eyes fixed on the cloth flap that served the tent as a door. Ezra was reminded of a cat waiting patiently at a mousehole. A woman's laugh rang out, then the rumble of Yusef's voice. Should Ezra creep closer to the tent? Try to hear what they were saying? But then Negasi might see him. Who knew what would happen if he reported back to the Kizlar Agha that Ezra had followed him. He didn't want to lose his place with Reuven

Hekim or get Aunt Rachel in trouble. He didn't know which would be worse. Both were unthinkable. Negasi wasn't trying to get closer. He shifted once on his haunches and settled back into stillness. It occurred to Ezra that Muslim men didn't go visiting Muslim women as friends the way regular people, that is, Jewish people did. He still wasn't exactly sure what it was that women did with men, but he had gathered that it took a while. He settled down to wait, copying Negasi's posture as best he could.

* * * *

"I could not search properly, Excellency," Negasi said, "with the woman shrieking and commanding me to get the wretch out of her tent, and he spewing and cursing. He was indeed very ill. Perhaps in his desire to impress the woman, he unwisely took the whole of the magical substance. In any case, I could not find any nor a vessel that might have contained it. I brought him back to the Palace—discreetly, in a litter—and left him in Reuven Hekim's care."

"And the woman?" the Kizlar Agha asked.

"I paid her well," Negasi said, "and told her that if she speaks even one word of the night's events, she will die a terrible death. The same if she attempts to leave Istanbul or hide her tent from the all-seeing eyes of the Sublime One's emissary, the Kizlar Agha, and his servants."

"You have done well, Negasi," the Kizlar Agha said.

He could do nothing more until Kira Rachel completed her investigation. He waited impatiently for the three days he had promised her to pass.

"Before you speak," he said, "I must tell you that I had Vizier Yusef followed. Let me tell you what my servant found."

Rachel listened attentively as he recounted Negasi's findings.

"If we need the woman to bear witness," he said, "we can easily retrieve her. I have also ordered a more rigorous search of her premises for the missing horn. Negasi thought Yusef was trying to impress her, but she is just a cheap woman who sells herself for pleasure. It is more likely that he was motivated by curiosity and envy. If Ibrahim Pasha had it, Yusef must have it first. If Ibrahim Pasha took a pinch, Yusef must have all of it, even though it made him sick as a dog."

"Dear *effendi*," Rachel said, "your reasoning is impeccable, based on the information you have. However, I have learned some details that you were not in a position to know. I hope you will not take offense."

"Of course not!" the Kizlar Agha said quickly. "As you say, we are in this together."

"Absolutely. You know that my nephew Ezra is studying with Reuven Hekim along with your eunuch Enis?"

The Kizlar Agha raised his eyebrows. He curled his finger around the heron feather in his turban for reassurance and nodded for her to continue.

"He followed Negasi the other night, hoping to be of use. *Please* do not mind. Physicians take a solemn oath to reveal nothing they know or see to anyone, and in fact, as you will see, his presence was fortunate for us. He waited outside the tent along with Negasi, who remained unaware of his presence, is that not so? He saw the commotion when Yusef became ill and came staggering out. Now, you said there was a further search of the woman's premises. The horn was never found, was it?"

"It was not." The Kizlar Agha tapped the curling toe of his soft leather slipper on the thickly carpeted floor. "I am being patient, *kira*."

"And I am grateful, *effendi*. You will understand in a moment. I don't know if you are aware, *effendi*, that in the Jewish religion, unlike Islam, wine is considered a sacrament. Thus our children see their elders drink alcohol from earliest childhood. We even have one festival, Purim, when Jews are actually instructed to get so drunk we 'cannot tell Mordecai from Haman'—the hero and the villain of the tale we celebrate that day. So what Negasi could not discern was obvious to Ezra. Yusef had not overindulged in unicorn horn. He was drunk. Reuven Hekim will confirm it. The *hekims* have saved some of his vomitus, reeking of alcohol, as evidence."

* * * *

"Good Muslims do not drink wine or spirits, do they, *hekim*?" Ezra asked.

"They do not," Reuven said.

"So Vizier Yusef must be a bad Muslim."

"That is not our business. He is our patient, and doctors swear a sacred oath to keep our patients' secrets."

"I cannot keep secrets from my master, the Kizlar Agha," Enis said.

"That is understood, Enis," Reuven said gently. "If there is need, and he commands you, do as you must."

Too late, Ezra thought. *I have already told Aunt Rachel, and she is telling the Kizlar Agha. But Reuven Hekim knows nothing of the missing remedy or of the danger to Enis, and he must not. He does not even know that Luljeta exists.*

"If the Sultan knew," Ezra said, "would he not be very angry with Yusef? Therefore, what might Yusef do to us who know of his behavior? He would only mock our sacred oath."

"True, Ezra," Reuven said, "he has rank and power and would make a dangerous enemy. It is fortunate that alcohol in large quantities carries the blessing of forgetfulness. In addition, I gave him poppy to soothe his tormented stomach. I guarantee that he awakened this morning in his own bed, having forgotten the woman, the forbidden spirits, and us."

* * * *

"So Yusef never had the unicorn horn," the Kizlar Agha said. "Then who did?"

"Let us consider the suspects," Rachel said. "Enis had it but no motive to keep it. Nermin had access to it on the afternoon she fled. But did she know where it was hidden? Its value? What it looked like? I suggest she did not. Neither Enis nor Nermin have any idea how unicorn horn is used. I myself heard Enis say, 'What use could a *hatun* possibly have for unicorn horn?' And Nermin told me that when the *hatuns* laughed about it, she did not understand the jokes. She arrived in the harem *after* Hürrem became the Sultan's Favorite and thus has never been trained in the arts of the bedchamber."

"I deduce you know our runaway better than you have admitted, *kira*."

"Yes, *effendi*," she said, "but you must forgive me, since I am about to name the true culprit. But first you must promise me my reward."

The Kizlar Agha scowled.

"You try me, *kira*. Let me guess. You are going to ask for her freedom."

"She never had the horn," Rachel said. "And she is of no value to the Sultan, who wants no woman but Hürrem in his bed. Cease your pursuit."

"Tell me truthfully: Is she under your roof now?"

"No, *effendi*." Rachel had confided her to Joanna's care in anticipation of this very question.

"What makes you so sure of her ignorance regarding the horn?"

"Everyone speaks of the *horn* of a unicorn. But those who have seen it know that the remedy is a powder ground from the horn and carried in a small vial. Nermin asked how she would hide the horn of an animal as big as a horse about her person. She had no reason to dissemble. The culprit is someone else. Who else had access to the vial once it left Enis's hands?"

"Everyone in the *haremlik* that afternoon," he said. "All the *hatuns* and their attendants."

"I agree," she said. "All the *hatuns*, who never leave, and every maidservant and eunuch who was on duty that afternoon could have taken the vial from the trunk as long as the lid remained open. But who had a motive, and what might that motive have been?"

"I am sure you are going to tell me," he said.

"Let me tell you the story of a *hatun* and a eunuch," Rachel said.

"One of *my* eunuchs? I refuse to—"

"No, no, *effendi*," Rachel said. "Not one of yours. Be patient but a little longer. You have served four Sultans. Have you ever encountered a *haseki* like Hürrem, with the power to captivate a Sultan for so long?"

"Never."

"So *hatuns* who expected a share of royal attention and a chance of bearing a future Sultan must feel cheated."

"When the *hatuns* are not content, one can feel the *haremlik*'s uneasiness."

"Which of all the *hatuns* is the most resentful?" Rachel asked. "One who got one taste of being the chosen one and wanted more."

"Aysun," he said. "She has been soured by discontent for quite some time."

"Aysun Hatun used to show the world her necklace from the Sultan," Rachel said. "Now she does not. Perhaps she fears drawing Hürrem's attention. But I do not think it is about bedgifts."

"She cannot have the Sultan."

"She wants a man," Rachel said.

"*Kira*, to speak bluntly," he said, "all the eunuchs in the *haremlik* are like me, deprived of every portion of our manhood."

"*Effendi*," she said, "I think she somehow found a eunuch in the Kapi Agha's service, a eunuch of the *selamlik*."

"A white eunuch!" he exclaimed. "Of course! They are only partly cut. They retain that which could pleasure a woman, so they are not allowed to serve in the *haremlik*. And that is why she wanted the ground unicorn horn—so he could be a man for her. How did she manage that, I wonder? Not the powder, but the intrigue? How did they meet? *Where* did they meet? We grow lax. Discipline must be tightened. But first, I will find this unruly eunuch and bring that wicked girl to heel. I warn you, *kira*, this will not end happily for them."

* * * *

Within a day, with the Kapi Agha's cooperation, they had the culprits in custody and the vial of powdered unicorn horn back in the *hekim*'s storeroom, for however meretricious the remedy, the Grand Vizier still wanted it. Under protest, Reuven Hekim put it into Ibrahim Pasha's hand himself, having been told enough of the story to appreciate the importance of impressing the bridegroom with a plausible rigmarole.

"Only the tiniest pinch will be efficacious, Excellency," he said. "The chief virtue lies in the spell, which is written on papyrus and must be soaked in this rare scented oil"—he solemnly offered the bridegroom another small vial—"and burned without reading before, er, before the event in question."

* * * *

"Tell me about the eunuch, *effendi*," Rachel said.

"The eunuch's name is Mochtil. A Bulgarian—the usual sad story, a boy who with good luck instead of bad would have ended up in the Palace school instead of the slave market. The slavemaster took a fancy to him, so when he was cut, he was left enough to use. He had friends among my eunuchs, and unauthorized visits took place. This should not have happened. It is my responsibility. My disgrace. If I had honor, I would tell the Sultan the whole story and bare my neck for the bowstring. But I confess, *kira*, that in my old age I have grown fond of life. I no longer dream of the African forest of my youth and the virility I lost. I cherish my quiet evenings with a volume of Rumi and a plate of Turkish delight."

"Does he show any interest in Aysun's fate?" she asked.

"You want to know if he loves her," the Kizlar Agha said. "Oh, he was fond enough of her. He was grateful to her for perceiving him as a man. Do you think I don't understand that? She, of course, had woven a fairytale and still believes it. Leyla and Mecnun. Very well, *kira*. For your sake, I will allow the two lovebirds to die in each other's arms.

And you may have the little runaway as a gift. I will tell the Sultan she was burned beyond recognition in the fire. But you cannot save them all."

✗

Elizabeth Zelvin's short stories have appeared in *Black Cat Mystery Magazine*, *Ellery Queen's Mystery Magazine*, and *Alfred Hitchcock's Mystery Magazine*. Nominated three times each for the Derringer and Agatha awards, she's edited anthologies *Me Too: Crimes Against Women, Retribution, and Healing* (September 2019) and *Where Crime Never Sleeps*. Her series are the Bruce Kohler Mysteries and the Mendoza Family Saga.

DON'T DO THAT

GIL BREWER

He shook his finger at his son.

"Just remember," he said. "Never touch that gun. A gun is a deadly thing, Bobby. Hands off."

"Why?"

"Because I said so. Guns make a big noise."

Bobby grinned. "Bang-bang!"

"That's right. So, hands off. Hear?"

Bobby looked longingly at the gun on the desk.

"Now, run along and play."

He helped Bobby from his study with gentle pats on the shoulder. Then he closed the door, returned to his desk and sat down.

They would never execute a six-year-old boy for the accident of murder.

From the moment Fred Ordway thought of this, he got into a highly nervous state and remained that way. Right now he was perspiring freely. He mopped his face, loosened his tie, and opened the window beside his desk.

It was a rotten way to work things out, but it was the only way. He'd planned and schemed any number of ways. It always ended with the one simple answer.

He looked at it logically. It didn't help. His wife, Marge, was beautiful, true—in a crystal-eyed, winey sort of way. But he liked martinis. He loved his son, Bobby. He had it soft, working only because it looked better. Marge had enough money so he would never have to work.

He was a real estate investigator, office in his home.

The only trouble was, he didn't love his wife. He loved his secretary. Passionately. He couldn't stand being in the same house with his wife. Yet, he loved his son. If he got a divorce, everything would come out into the open. Marge would gain custody of Bobby. He would lose the house and the money.

True, he would have Lillian. But how much better it would be to have Lillian *and* the money *and* Bobby.

Lillian liked Bobby. Bobby liked Lillian.

And Marge was a mess, even if she was Bobby's mother.

He could not bear to lose the money. He was sick of real estate investigating. Marge didn't suspect a thing concerning Lillian.

There was only the one thing to do.

Kill Marge.

So when he thought of the *how*, it floored him. He didn't know whether it would work. But he became obsessed with the need to try.

He would be absolutely in the clear.

If it worked, Bobby would forget.

"Fred?" It was Marge, outside the study door. She opened the door and looked at him. "Miss Joyce isn't back from downtown yet?"

He shook his head. "Miss Joyce" was Lillian. "She had to pick up some papers."

"Oh," Marge said. "Anyway, I've got to run down to the church. About the bazaar."

"All right."

"Keep an eye on Bobby?"

"Sure."

He grinned at Marge. She smiled back at him. Her eyes were a very deep blue and they were striking, along with the shoulder-length auburn hair. She was wearing a fresh white linen suit, with large ebony buttons, and as he stared at her there in the doorway, he wished momentarily that what was happening hadn't. She was quite beautiful.

Well, he thought, that's life.

"See you then," Marge said.

"Right. Uh—Bobby and I might go out for a while. Case we're gone when you get back."

"Oh? Where?"

"I'm going to do a little shooting. Break the monotony. Out to the sand pits." He gestured toward the gun.

"With Bobby?"

"I'd like him to get used to guns, Marge. You know."

"Well, you be careful."

"Sure."

"I gotta run—bye!"

He listened to her heels smack smartly down the hall. The front door closed. He heard her crunching on the gravel in the drive. A car door slammed. She drove off.

He sat there, musing—perspiring. He had to keep his mind closed to the fact of what he was planning. It wasn't easy. Why couldn't things in life be solved more easily? There should be a provision.

Lillian knew nothing of what he intended. He did not want her to know.

He picked up the gun. It was a .32 Savage automatic. Light enough for Bobby to handle, yet not obviously so. He had to watch the obvious. He had worked on it himself. It reacted to a gentle touch of the trigger finger. It was a fine, deadly little gun.

He took three boxes of shells from his desk drawer, then put one back. The thing was to whip up desire in Bobby, but not to overdo it. It would be bad if Bobby became tired of the gun.

Ordway knew he wouldn't. He knew Bobby. The way Bobby's mind worked, the way he reacted to things, had tipped him off in the first place.

He put the boxes of shells in his pocket, and was about to hunt his son, when a car turned in the drive. He could tell it was Lillian by the sound of her walking.

He met her in the hall.

"She's not home?" Lillian said.

"No."

"Oh, honey," Lillian said. She moved in close to him, laid the bundle of papers she was carrying on the hall table, and kissed him. Holding Lillian was like handling fused, loose dynamite to Ordway. She did crazy things to him that he had never experienced before. Whenever he touched her bright blonde hair, he went a little mad inside. She twisted and writhed in his arms. She was never still. She was wearing a tight aqua dress of some material that slid loosely against her firm body and her warm lips more than threatened his sanity. "Honey, honey—gee!" she said.

"Daddy!" Bobby called, running through the living room.

Lillian jumped back, staring at Ordway with round amber eyes that seemed to spin as he looked at her. Her hands were trembling and so were his. Not touching, he could feel an actual vibration, like electricity, flowing between them.

He had been reeling with this feeling ever since he'd first met Lillian. It compensated for whatever he planned. Two human beings who were meant for each other as much as Lillian and he shouldn't allow anything to stand in their way. It was a natural law.

"I just—just can't even talk," Lillian said.

"Daddy!"

"I'm the same way," he told her. "Listen. I've got to take Bobby out. I promised him."

Bobby came up to him, took his hand.

Lillian placed her white upper teeth across her full lower lip and stood there with one hand against the side of her face. She nodded. "All right, Fred." She picked up the papers, brushed against him as she moved down the hall toward the study. He almost weakened. "To-night, then."

He swallowed sharply. "Tonight."

She closed the study door.

He took Bobby into the other room.

"How'd you like to go shooting with me?" he said. He brought the gun out of his pocket, showed it to Bobby, put it away again.

Bobby's eyes enlarged and began to shine.

"Good," Ordway said. "Fine!"

* * * *

"Don't ever point it at your mother," Ordway said. "Mustn't scare women. Understand? You know how women are."

Bobby nodded briskly, watching the gun in Ordway's hand. Bobby was terribly excited, his face pale.

Ordway looked at his son. He shrugged his shoulders against a sudden feeling of bright guilt and turned toward a close bank, where there was a row of tin cans. The sand pits were a mile or so out of town, in a spotty pine woods, well hidden from the highway. He had thoroughly inspected the area to make certain no one was around. A lot of folks came here for practice shooting. The ground was littered with spent shells. Riddled targets lay everywhere. In the deep depressions between the hummocks and slopes of sand, large ponds of water stagnated. Frogs jumped, and the noon wind breathed among the pines, moaning softly.

"You hold it like this," he said. "But don't ever point it at Mama, Bobby. It would scare her to hear so much noise. Don't ever point it at your mother and scare her with the noise." He turned quickly, and aimed at the tin cans. "Don't ever take the gun from my desk and point it at your mother, or anybody! Don't shoot it!"

He squeezed the trigger as fast as he could. The magazine emptied in a continuous roaring explosion. His ears rang. The gun bucked in his hand.

Bobby laughed hysterically, leaping up and down.

"Bang! Bang!" Bobby yelled.

"You must never do that to your mother, Bobby. You know how women are about guns. They're afraid of guns. They aren't like men." He loaded the magazine again, as he talked. "For instance," he said, "if that was Mama standing right there in front of us. My, would she be scared if you pointed the gun at her—and pulled the trigger." He fired two shots.

Bobby laughed. Ordway laughed. He slapped Bobby on the back.

"See?" he said. "Mama would be scared if you shot at her. Don't ever point the gun at Mama and shoot," he cried, pointing the gun at the imaginary image of Marge. He emptied the magazine again.

"Let me!" Bobby said.

This was what he'd been waiting for.

"You must never touch this gun," he said. "Never take it from my desk, where it'll always be. Don't ever point it at anybody. Hear?"

Bobby was so excited he couldn't talk. He ran up and down and rolled on the sand, holding one finger in his ear. His ears were ringing, too.

"Let me," Bobby said, reaching for the gun. He tried to grab the gun.

Ordway laughed loudly. He pushed back at Bobby, letting his son touch the gun. Bobby grabbed the gun and tried to yank it out of Ordway's hand.

"Wait'll I load it." Ordway loaded the magazine again. "Now, don't ever point it at your mother. You must never touch the gun, hear? Never touch it!"

Bobby stood there, close to tears.

"Never touch the gun," Ordway said. "Here," he said, handing it to Bobby. "Now, don't shoot Mama!" he yelled.

Bobby turned toward the near bank, where imaginary Mama was, and squeezed the trigger until the magazine was empty. Bullets flew all over. Bobby roared with laughter.

"Don't shoot Mama!" Bobby cried.

"That's right," Ordway said. "Don't ever point the gun at Mama and shoot it. Don't ever touch the gun."

Bobby beamed at him.

"I'm a good shot," Bobby said.

"Yes," Ordway said. "Here. Let me load it for you." He took the gun, loaded the magazine. "Remember," he said. "A gun is always loaded—always. Don't ever touch this gun, where I keep it on the corner of my desk."

Bobby grabbed the gun.

"Don't point it at Mama, Bobby. Don't shoot it!"

Bobby fired the gun.

Ordway kept this up for the rest of the afternoon, until all the cartridges were gone. Bobby had a wonderful time. He laughed a lot and was very excited about it all.

Ordway was excited, too.

"Now, what must you remember?" Ordway said, driving home from the sand pits.

"Don't ever point the gun at anybody—Mama, or anybody," Bobby said. He swallowed. "Don't ever shoot it. Don't touch it, where you keep it on your desk."

"Don't ever touch the gun," Ordway said.

"Yes," Bobby said. He laughed. He pointed his finger at the dashboard. "Don't ever!" he said. "Bang! Bang!" he shouted.

They laughed together.

For several days they went out to the sand pits.

* * * *

Three weeks later, Ordway was watering the lawn and talking with Simmons, the next-door neighbor.

"How about a beer?" Ordway said. "The refrigerator's full up."

Simmons agreed that a beer would go well. It was a warm afternoon. They went to the house and entered at the kitchen door.

Marge was plastered up against the kitchen stove, making small noises with her mouth, staring with frightened eyes at Bobby.

"Good Lord!" Simmons said.

Bobby stood there with the gun pointed at her.

"A toy?" Simmons said.

"Fred," Marge whispered. "He's got your gun. He just keeps standing there, laughing to himself. Fred! Stop him. He's just a child. He doesn't know what he's doing."

"Yes," Ordway said. "Sure." He wanted to laugh, but after all, Simmons was with him. "Bobby," he shouted. "Don't shoot!"

Bobby laughed and squeezed the trigger until the magazine was empty. The explosions shattered the stillness of the house. He only missed his mother once, putting a neat hole through the coffee pot. Coffee spurted onto the stove.

Marge was dead before she struck the floor.

* * * *

"The child admits his father warned him never to point a gun at anybody," the coroner said during the post mortem. "Even, never to touch that gun."

"It's terrible," Ordway said. "What can I do?" He held his head in his hands, rocking it slightly from side to side.

"We cannot condemn a six-year-old child. Curiosity. It's tragic, but the boy doesn't know what he's done."

"Poor kid," Ordway said. "Poor Bobby."

"It can only be adjudged that Mrs. Ordway died as a result of a child's mistake."

Ordway closed his eyes.

"Our sympathies to you, Mr. Ordway."

"I'll smash the gun," Ordway said, standing up and shouting. "Smash it! Smash it, I tell you!"

* * * *

He didn't smash it. He put it at the bottom of his old Army duffle bag under some camping equipment, and stuck the duffle bag in the back of the garage.

For six months he did nothing about Lillian. Then they were married. Everybody was pleased to see Fred Ordway smiling and happily married again.

"This is your new mother, Bobby," Ordway said. "You like her?"

"Yes," Bobby said. "I love her."

Lillian never knew about things. She loved Fred deeply and honestly and with a passion that never died. Fred loved her the same way. They were truly meant for each other.

Sometimes he thought about Marge and what had happened, but he never experienced any real sense of loss.

After all, he had Lillian.

"Are you ever going to tell the boy the truth about what he did?" Lillian asked. "I mean, when he grows up?"

"I don't know," Ordway said. "It's tough."

Bobby didn't laugh about it. He missed Marge. He had loved his mother a great deal.

"It's all right," Ordway said. "Your mother went away. You've got a nice new Mama now."

Bobby smiled and went out to play.

* * * *

A week later, Ordway was in the garage, hunting for the oil can, so he could get the power mower to running just right. He noticed his army duffle bag dragged out on the floor.

"My God," he said.

He rushed into the house.

"Lillian!"

Lillian was over against the living room wall. She screamed soundlessly, her hands clenched in front of her.

Bobby had the gun. "Look, Daddy. I found it."

"No," Ordway whispered. "Don't do that, Bobby." He tried to creep up on his son.

Bobby laughed. He fired the gun three times at Lillian.

"Don't shoot Mama!" Bobby shouted.

Lillian sprawled on the floor, dead.

Ordway leaped at Bobby, something inside him screaming crazily. Bobby turned, laughing, and emptied the magazine into his father's chest.

"Don't shoot anybody!" Bobby yelled.

✗

Gilbert "Gil" Brewer (1922-1983) was an American novelist and short story author. He was born in Canandaigua, New York After leaving the army at the end of World War II, Brewer joined his family, who had settled in St. Petersburg, Florida. There he met his future wife, Verlaine, and he married her in 1947.

Brewer started by writing serious novels, but soon turned to pulp paperbacks after a sale to Gold Medal Books in 1950. At one point, he had five books on the stands. Unwilling to promote himself, his career took a turn for the worse after a mental breakdown, and a long decline into alcoholism.

He is best remembered these days as a noir crime writer whose novels included *Satan Is a Woman* (Gold Medal, 1951); *So Rich, So Dead* (Gold Medal, 1951); *13 French Street* (Gold Medal, 1951); *Flight to Darkness* (Gold Medal, 1952), and *Hell's Our Destination* (Gold Medal, 1953). Wildside Press has reprinted many of his short stories from *Manhunt* magazine.